Things of the Flesh
An urban horror collection

Jennifer Rachel Baumer

Monstrosity Ink

Reno, Nevada

Things of the Flesh
An urban horror collection

ISBN – 13: 978-0615973609 (Monstrosity Ink)
ISBN – 10: 0615973604

Monstrosity Ink

Contents

Things of the Flesh was originally written for a horror anthology dealing with road stories and cars. The anthology never got published, but somehow spawned a sequel (I'm not sure how that works) that was going to be called Killers on the Road, a line from The Doors song "Riders on the Storm."
That anthology never got published either.
But Things of the Flesh is such a vicious little story, it needed to see the light of day somewhere—maybe it will turn to ash like a vampire?

Things of the Flesh

This side of Independence the car starts making an unhealthy sound, like a cat with a hairball or like Timmy right before we decided a little boy like him was more trouble than we needed and ditched him outside social services in some half-assed town in Michigan.

Bess pulls to the side of the road and makes a sound that kind of echoes what the car did, only hers is all fury and aggravation. "Well. What the hell am I supposed to do now?" she demands and she's not waiting for any kind of answer because she definitely does not know I'm along for the ride. Bess and I had a falling out some 300 miles ago and I went stalking off into the night in my little skirt and spike heels, supremely confident in my anger and never guessing that just around the corner I'd meet somebody that much bigger and meaner than me. Police found my bodies two days later and they're still trying to piece together who I am– or was– but by then I was far away riding with Bess and Bess doesn't even know enough to be upset, past her own fury with me– doesn't even realize I'm dead.

So when the car calls it quits this side of Independence and Bess makes those teakettle noises that always did mean she was about to boil over, there's no way for her to know I'm there with her. Or that I've brought company. All along the way we've been passing ghosts, hungry ghosts, angry ones– and I've been inviting them to come with because honestly, just listening to Bess berate me hasn't been that much fun. The others, she's long past taking it out on them. They're old news. They're history. They're towns and stops before I came along and seems I lasted longer than most of them before going the way of most of Bess's ex's and we found each other easily, as if there were a call, came together to form some sort of sisterhood, not that I ever had a sister but maybe it's not too late now.

And our latest rider, she has a knife, and a wicked gleam in her eyes– or what used to be her eyes before– and she says, just says, mind you, that there is a way to interact with the living, that you really can reunite for old times sake, and I think tonight we're going to find out.

The bar is crowded. Bess would head somewhere like this. No clue what she means to do or if she's already done it. Maybe the car's in the shop, maybe she had it towed and paid the driver in flesh and now she's killing time. Or maybe we've lost time again, it seems to happen, the way everything seems to move along in fits and starts, or jolts and clumps.

The bar is crowded, past fire code regulations, past human endurance. The senses are assaulted – Old Spice is prevalent (doesn't it *ever* go out of style?) along with every other scent. The smell of human flesh rendering, scorched leather, burnt rope and the funny chemical scent of the new inhalants (Summer Sky was my favorite for sheer, stunning vertigo pleasure but that's behind me now.) Halfway across the floor Bess is holding court. That's what it looks like, anyway. She's holding her drink which wouldn't dare spill on her even though she's thrown her head back and abandoned herself to laughter. Whatever drugs pumps beneath her surface, it's left her skin shiny and lickable. Except licking isn't what I intend to do to her.

I circle around her, me and my new friends, and Sheila has the knife out. Been a long couple days since the time I found myself in that alley and when I thought about going back inside of – well, me – realized it was a little too thoroughly vacated, a few too many holes – a real fixer upper, you might say, and no way to take possession.

I left it there and went to find Bess and it was about then I started to remember everything: the way I'd stormed away from the club because Bess was coming on to everyone but me, the person she'd come with, and I thought I was more than just a bed warmer. And the way I'd gone off into the night and into that alley, more out of fury than anything else. I'd show her, I'd put something she cared about at risk. Only it was supposed to be a symbolic risk, not literal, and I wasn't supposed to go around that corner and find something bigger and meaner than me. And even if all those things happened anyway, the bigger, meaner thing around the corner wasn't supposed to be Bess.

So now I'm back and she's here and Sheila has shown me how to break free and the only question is where to begin and how fast the packed dance floor will empty out when disembodied hands yank Bess's head back and start cutting along her neck.

"Not yet," Sheila says and takes the knife and I just look at her, all fury and holes and the need to use Bess's blood and flesh to fill them. For a minute I want to hurt Sheila but Bess has already been there, done that. I search Sheila's good eye and the others swarm around us. There's about a dozen but some of them have lost so much coherence it's hard to count them any more, hard to consider them a number. There's a bunch closer together, though; newer, fresher. Angrier. They're around Sheila now, angry as I am, but she stands her ground while around us the club shimmies and shakes and sways and burns and Bess floats her hands down one slender form, one then another, her lips parted and eyes lidded and come on.

"Not yet?" I mean to sound threatening, tough. I was with Bess. I ran with her. I lasted longer than a lot of them. But the words slide from my lips like a petulant child denied a treat. Like Timmy denied the car when we left him at social services and he was too stupid to know the gift she was giving him. And the others ran with Bess, too, it's not such a distinction, and Bess only knows two kinds of women and Sheila is not a prettygirl. She is, after all, the one with the knife, the one with the plan. The one who knows how to get beyond the things of the flesh and interact with the living.

On the dance floor Bess throws her head back again and laughs at something somebody said, or just for the hell of it, or because of the drugs inside her, or because it makes her hair more glorious, that liquid silk of gold down her spine and the girl she's seducing is glazed and dazed and halfway there already. Bess is vain about her hair, she uses it to lure the unwary and trap the unsuspecting, a medusa who coils her victims in her shining tresses.

My hands tangle briefly in her hair and I pull, watch her eyes water and fists harden, but there's no one very close to her, she can't tell who did it. She moves back to the sweet young thing in front of her, so vapid, so wasted on drugs there's no way we can't act tonight – if that sweet young dustbunny joins our cadre I'll be forcing Bess to drive into a wall at speed, just to get free. If I can force Bess to do anything.

And it's worth a try but Sheila says just wait as if she knows what I'm thinking and probably she does. The others are all around us, Angela and Sunny and Kims and the ones who are echoes and too far gone to remember names, only bits of blue eyes or dark hair or pouting lips. And fury.

Bar closes at two. I used to think that was early. Now it seems very late. It's been a long night, watching Bess play her prey, waiting to see which she'd cull from the herd, waiting to see what Sheila would say. She knows something, somehow, Sheila. As if she's gone on or gone farther than the rest of us and returned. And she needs me, enough to give me the lead and let me play some, enough that when the time comes it'll be her knife but my hands. Maybe because I'm newest. Freshest. Still the most alive or at least the one who still best remembers what that means. Another reason to act tonight– if Bess takes on that Bambi she'll be top girl. I can't see it.

Long night watching Bess and missing the feel of lights and heat and the sweat breaking when the adrenal drugs kick in. Long night and once the bartender caught sight of me in the mirror and turned to ask – "What's your poison?" – already on his lips even as his brain tracked I couldn't possibly drink, anything I took would flow through the red of my neck and when he turned I was gone – for him – and when he turned back to the mirror again he only got a glimpse. I would have thought it would scare him straight. Or at least sober. Perhaps it did the latter, but maybe he liked what he saw, maybe he's someone sick and lost, because rather than run for a church or a priest or a gun and swear off the hard stuff, he slapped another TransD patch on his neck alongside the old one, lips moving without sound like an old time incantation along with a newfangled patch would protect him from evil.

Thought I was the victim here but maybe he saw something I didn't.

"It's coming," Laura or Amy whispers. Their hands on my arms are cold and wet and only partially there, as if they could slide into my flesh. I shrug them off and stand with Sheila outside the club. Moon's up, stars. Even with the city lights you can see that. Gory lurid neons catch in Bess's hair as she exits with the Bambi and I'm pretty sure now– Bambi's not a runner, not a companion or sidekick, Bambi's one of the drifting, smoky ones. I've had some time to think about it, to look at our hierarchy of sisterhood– those who ran with Bess, those who tried to run from her. The short term relationships and the no term. The ones who walked from the club the winner of some obscure popularity contest, the trophy on Bess's arm or perhaps she was the trophy, and when they woke it was to find they'd never wake again. They were the misty ones, the others among all of us who are only others, swept up and cast aside and always at the answer to Bess's whim.

"Easy," Sheila breathes but I've had it with caution and going slow. If there's a way to bridge the gap between the living and the sisterhood, I want to find it.

We slide into the car with them, spectators at the feast. The girl's eyes are wide and clear and innocent and so guileless I can almost believe for a minute that she's conning Bess, that the tables will turn and the balance tip but no, she is only a doe-eyed innocent, sure in her place as she dips her head and allows Bess to nip at her wrist, sharp at first, then harder until she breaks the skin, some kind of ritual for her. I still bear the scar though logic tells me I can wish it away, change my form to whatever I choose, I choose to stay the way Bess will recognize me when I come.

The girl bows her head and Bess's tongue flickers along her neck and collarbones, all the while her hands pulling her own clothes aside, rearranging it to suit herself, inviting the girl down to nip and suck and the knife is in her hand as if it were born there.

"Easy, slow. Easy."

I don't need Sheila's guidance, I only need her knife, watching for the moment to slip inside, for the opening to be made and the chance to act.

Time flips, or maybe I just lose a bit of it, unable to watch the girl's tongue on Bess's skin, not that I hadn't thought there'd been others before me, just that I hadn't expected to lose so much so soon. Bess shudders and her legs tighten and trap and the knife comes up and in a moment it's almost already too late. The knife drags across the girl's flat stomach, thin line, preliminary cut, enough to send her Lycra-laced t-shirt sliding open and a thin red line across her skin. It's almost not enough of a gap but Bambi's not having any of it, she fights back harder than I would have expected, clawing, fighting, biting. Her teeth and nails are formidable and somebody taught her to punch. Bess takes a blow to the jaw that rocks her head back; her teeth snap together when her head hits the window and her instant's inattention is all I need. I hear Sheila whisper *go* even as I'm already sliding inside, swollen with desire and delirious at having flesh around me again, a moment lost to the wonder of being, of the body, flesh and blood and tidal sway of heartbeat, stale breath and quickening cut of adrenaline and just-lapsed orgasm. A moment's confusion from Bess and the Bambi jumps, hands to her stomach, hands to the door, almost gets it open and then the hands are around her throat and the joy is singing inside me as I sing inside her, the hunt, the prey, the capture, the kill. I tighten Bess's hands around the girl's thin white neck and squeeze until she's loose and uncomplicated, no resistance, nothing but fear and the beginnings of loss.

I can feel the others around me, Sheila with her knife, the Amys and Angelas and Corys and all, feel them pushing up and rising inside, crowding out Bess until there's nowhere left for her, no room, no residual high. Until the kill is ours, until we've taken from her as she has taken from us.

It's good to be flesh again. Good to smell blood and stink and fear. Good to feel Bess pummeling me and the Bambi struggle under my thumbs against her windpipe and Sheila's knife against her throat. Time winds down and there is only the running, Bess leaving the body behind a warehouse as the sun threatens and dawn lights the badlands. I no longer know where we are. I'm sated, and content to let Bess carry us away, the passengers she doesn't know she carries, predators and prey moving over red-lit blacktop as the sun rises.

Bess drives in single minded fury. There's not even room for confusion. She was cheated out of a kill and she can't figure out how, and maybe if she glanced in the rearview right now she'd see us, bloated and dozy with what we've done but she drives looking forward and away from the night and the sisterhood dreams of things of the flesh.

Stone, and Brass started life as a freewriting exercise and grew into a creepy short story, incorporating elements from years of nightmares about graves for the living. In April 2005, Editor John Benson included it in his beautiful magazine Not One of Us.

Stone, and Brass

In the evenings, Stella's brain was free to do whatever it liked. She could think or not think, plan or not plan. She hummed to herself sometimes without any worry of remembering the rest of the song and she forgot about her fears: whether she actually might have brain damage, whether she might actually be crazy and imagining everything. Whether or not she was actually safe here.

In the evenings, Stella washed dishes and glasses, glasses of all descriptions, glasses with lipstick smears and glasses with cigar butts wedged down in them and glasses whose contents no one had touched. She stood in the back of Mac's and washed glasses and stared out the huge window over the double metal wash bins into the alley beyond.

From here there really wasn't much of a view. She could see into the alleyway behind the bar across ten feet to the fence where her view stopped. She could see the trash cans and the dumpsters and the place where the bartenders and waitresses took smoke breaks. Sometimes she saw crows or seagulls or dogs. But most of the time the alley was empty and Stella's thoughts could be reined in by the fence or fly free over it.

When she got off shift at one a.m., Stella would head out the back door past the bartenders and waitresses. Sometimes they'd exchange pleasantries and sometimes they'd all just nod. It was all surface anyway, and therefore all somehow comforting. She knew their first names; only the owner knew her last name. She liked it that way. Stella would go past the trash cans and around the building to the side and climb a flight of sure-to-be-condemned wood stairs up to the apartment above the bar.

As she went up the stairs she could look between the risers at a brown cardboard box that was decaying in the winter slush and rains. She never stopped and went behind the staircase to see what was in it. She was saving that, holding it in reserve. As long as she didn't look in the box it could hold all manner of mysteries or treasures.

Once upstairs in the tiny apartment with the voices and music and television from the bar coming through the walls and sleep impossible until everything closed at three and the television programmed for static or sex, she'd stand at her own sink, one story up from where she washed dishes in Mac's. From upstairs she had more of a view, more than just trash cans and fence. From here she could see across the alley and over the fence, across the street and just into the cemetery beyond.

She'd never gone there, either, never asked anyone about it. Like the box under the stairs, she was saving it, keeping it in reserve for some day more empty than the others. On that day she'd walk across the alley and let herself through the gate in the fence, cross the avenue and go inside the wrought iron gates into the cemetery.

She was afraid that day would come, a day so empty or dull or full of dread she could no longer bear the day-to-day existence she'd dreamed up for herself.

Stella didn't want to face that day.

"Where are you from?" Gina perched on the edge of the steel sink, tiny little thing all of about 95 pounds, gamine and cute with her ponytail and white shorts. She wore shorts all winter long because she said her legs got her better tips and she might as well make the best of it while she was young. Gina was cute in a Barbie kind of way, with a matching IQ, and Stella liked her but she wasn't sure she wanted to really get to know anyone around Mac's and she definitely didn't want to be known by anyone.

"Originally San Francisco," she said. "Born and raised." And she talked a little about the fog and the bridges and the people before she asked Gina about Gina and in that way managed to avoid But where are you from *recently*? How did you get *here*? As if here – little desert town in Northern California – was so very bad.

There were many other places that could be much worse.

Gina's questions awakened the beast, though. That night the dreams started again and Stella rolled and flailed and protested on the lumpy pull-out bed in the tiny apartment over Mac's and across from the cemetery. She dreamed of Frank, till-death-do-us-part Frank and in the dreams she was no more able to dodge the blows than she had been in real life.

All those years, apparently she'd been cataloging the isolated incidents as Frank always called them. Each and every isolated incident played out in her nocturnal mind, blow by blow, split lip, black eye, permanent hearing damage. Over and over in the dream she told Gina, "Hell. I'm from Hell. I used to live in Hell. But I'm supposed to be safe here." Gina sat on the sink in Stella's old kitchen – that beautiful, rambling kitchen with brick around the oven and copper pans hanging over the stove and all the sunlight in the afternoons – and nodded and smiled and said, "But really, Stella, where are *you* from?" As if she couldn't hear Stella. As if she didn't believe her.

As if Stella wasn't there.

The next day Stella woke at eight. Not enough sleep but the dream – downgraded from nightmare status but still horrible and relentless – refused to end and she was more tired of it than tired and so she got up and fixed herself coffee and toast and stood at the sink where she could see across the alley into the cemetery beyond.

She imagined the gravestones, the angels, the mausoleum, imagined flowers and trinkets and letters left on graves and tended by family. She imagined all the undone things and unsaid words, unfinished lives and undreamed dreams buried in the ground across the way and shivered, her bare feet cold against the worn linoleum, glad for the space heater the owner provided. Wasn't that the tragedy of cemeteries? Not the burying of pasts but the loss of futures?

She'd buried her past.

She wrapped the coffee cup in cold fingers and closed her eyes and breathed in the steam. The dream pricked the edges of her mind. She'd buried her past. Left everything behind. Her job, her bookstores where she went for coffee and to talk about the new releases with the clerks. Her friends, at work, the ones she walked with on breaks, had lunch with or bitch sessions after work over margaritas. She'd left her house and her friends, the ones you called when something was really wrong. The ones she couldn't call because something was really wrong. She'd left her kids – Julie and her new husband and her new baby and Frank Jr, at college, free and safe, she could only hope.

Don't, she told herself, but she did it anyway, went to her purse and pulled out the battered packet, half a dozen postcards and letters before she grew too afraid to answer, before she had to stop running/moving for a while and therefore couldn't answer because he might find out.

Might. Would.

"Mama, please. Please come home. Call us. Let us know you're all right. We all love you so much. Please come home." Julie's beautiful writing, a little ragged, and the ink stained and smeared as if she'd cried. Stella had almost called when that post card came, she was already on the run, had doubled back to pick up mail, already another town down the line. But she read on. And stopped. And stared, unbelieving, at what she read.

She'd gone on the run for good then, traded in her car, taken, definitely, by the used car lot, but she'd had to get rid of the family car. In the cold, in the battered Ford with the heater that didn't work and the fog in that bleak coastal day she'd reread the rest of Julie's card. "Mama, please. We'll all help. Daddy said he'll help. We'll get you all the help you need, it's all right, we understand. Nobody blames you. It's probably physical, chemical, everything you believe, everything you said about Daddy—"

And yes, Stella supposed. It was physical after all. She still bore bruises over her kidneys, still saw blood when she went to the bathroom and Julie, darling Julie, telling her how much they all missed her and they'd help her.

Help her past her mental illness, apparently. How well Frank had played them. How much they loved their father. How little will she had left to fight with.

She put the letters away. *That's where I'm from*, she thought. *From life. Into death. I liked my life, my children, my friends, my job at the library, my new grandchild, my house. I didn't want to wash dishes in a bar called Mac's and live upstairs over the bar, but I didn't want to die, either.*

She'd moved back to the window, stood staring at the sleet and the dark day outside, her vision soft and unfocused. But *I didn't want to die* brought her back and she surfaced and found herself watching across the alley where the crows lit on the spiky iron fence around the cemetery, where she couldn't actually see any gravestones or structures or flowers and where, actually, she'd never seen anyone go.

Today was the day. Today at last was empty enough and desperate enough. Today she'd unwrap one of the mysteries.

The sleet started falling harder the minute she got to the bottom of the untrustworthy stairs and Stella shivered. All those coats back in her closets at home. She'd been on the run long enough the seasons had changed and her wardrobe was still something like two-week vacation style. She'd taken so very little. Photos of Julie and Frank Jr in her wallet. Toiletries. One bag of clothes. All the books she'd ever loved and hidden in. Turned her back on the rest. Left it for Frank to bury.

Sleet found its way down her collar and she thought about going back upstairs, maybe taking a bath towel or blanket to wrap up in. But she was on an adventure! she told herself and if she went back upstairs she'd end up next to the space heater with a book and the day would roll down to five p.m. and she'd need to go start washing glasses and looking out the window across the alley at the tiny adventure she'd skipped.

Stella pulled her collar tighter and headed across the alley, half ducking to avoid being noticed but there was no one in the alley smoking and no one came after her and she found herself contrarily wishing someone were out to call cheerily, "Hey, Stella! Where you off to?"

She felt unreal in the sleet, the leaden sky pressing earthward. The day was utterly silent, her footsteps muted. She felt like a ghost and when she reached the gate in the alley fence she turned and looked back at Mac's and the lighted windows made her feel lonely, and alone.

The other side of the fence lay a narrow avenue where cars rarely passed. The street in front of Mac's was a main street; this little avenue was a tributary. Almost directly across from her stood the filigree iron gates to the cemetery and she wondered which side – the cemetery or Mac's – had put the gate in the alley fence to facilitate access.

The gates to the cemetery were unlocked, ornate and icy under her hands and they didn't shriek in rusty protest as she pushed them open, which only served to make her feel more unreal.

It was only mid-afternoon but already streetlights along the avenue were blinking on, spreading tight circles of light that made the day seem darker once they were left behind.

Stella stepped into the graveyard and stood, breathing mystery.

There were no gravestones, she realized first with a start. What she couldn't see from her apartment over the bar – gravestones, plaster angels, crosses, mausoleums – she couldn't see because they weren't there. There were no crosses, no angels, no monuments, no marble, no flowers. Just row after row of checkerboard patches, winter dead grass and brass plaques set at definite, precise intervals.

It wasn't a military cemetery – there were no flags, no emblems and in this tiny nowhere desert town, no reason.

The wind picked up a little, blew cold and wet into her face and Stella blinked. Now that she was here there seemed little point. She wasn't a ghoul, she'd just imagined spending some time looking at ornate stones, ancient angels, cracked and crumbling legends of love. She'd feel sorrow for the children with their incomplete spans and amazed at the fancy stones that screamed "Notice me!" even in death. She'd give a wry smile for the inevitable wit who would have written "I told you I was sick" across his – or more likely – her stone.

But this. This graveyard was silence. This cemetery colored the day around it, reflected back the bleak and empty winter afternoon. It was neat and ordered, putting paid to people's chaotic, tumultuous lives.

Stella stepped away from the gate and the iron filigree swung the last few inches shut with the shriek she'd expected at the beginning. She jumped and glared at the offending gate and stepped into the graveyard itself.

Time stopped. There was only silence and swirling snow, wet and thick but turning fast from sleet to honest snow. She moved to the first row and knelt, looking at the plaque. She had wanted to dream other people's lives, so very different from her own. "Loving Wife and Mother" "Friend" "Lover" "Husband" "Wife".

The first plaque, aged brass, dull and tarnished, read "Jane Doe. 2002. Rest in Peace." Stella flinched as if from a blow. No life story. No life. No name, no idea how old she was. Just a lost girl name and a date of death and no story here, no life. She leaned to the next marker, John Doe, and two more following him. Some of them had dates of birth, most just listed dates of death. Stella rose on suddenly unsteady legs and passed through three rows, moving toward the center of the offensively neat grid. And now there were some names, first names, a rare last, some dates of origin as well as destruction and Stella wandered, reading, thinking, no longer aware of the snow that fell around her, brushing it off markers and reading names as if paying a penance, bringing their lives to life as penalty for burying her own.

She stopped in the most recent section, dates within the last couple years, and something warned her she didn't want to keep going, like that funny hot, tight, trembling feeling she'd get even before she walked through the front door and discovered Frank getting all worked up about something.

She knelt beside another plaque and read Tammie, and dates, too short, and then Bryan and Dave and Karen.

The trembling spread through her abdomen and into her bones and muscles. Her chest muscles spasmed and her teeth chattered and she knew she was crying but she couldn't stop. She knelt in the snow and frozen earth as the light leached from the day and she read the names of the waitresses and bartenders and the other dishwasher and the sometimes cook and Mac himself, who had taken her in and given her a safe place to stay, safe and warm with money and an identify if she wanted it but she'd refused. She was Stella, just Stella, afraid to claim her place in the world lest Frank come and rip her out of it.

She kept moving, slowly, on her hands and knees, one marker at a time, as she made her way down the most recent aisle.

Gina, she read, and her throat closed on tears. Little Gina in her shorts and ponytail. She didn't understand, only knew the fear was growing worse and she crawled to the next plaques, heart heavy and pounding hard against the cage of her chest. Tony, and she had to think, squirrely little guy, she'd seen him running errands for the bar, shifty guy who looked like he had no ties to hold him at all and consequently might do anything at any moment and apparently she'd got some of that right.

"Please," she said out loud as she passed to the last marker flush against the winter dirt in the dark winter graveyard. "Please no. Please."

The brass marker was empty. No names engraved, no stories untold, only the faintest whisper of something across the surface. No one lay beneath her feet, under the marker, lost forever with stories untold.

Her bones went loose and liquid. Stella pitched forward, hands against the dirt on either side of the marker and sobs shook her as past and present met and buffeted each other, and Stella sobbed for everything she'd lost, everything Frank had taken from her.

Everything she'd given up.

Gina came back in the middle of her shift, blew blond bangs out of her face and said "Phew! I think they're trying to kill me out there tonight." She hoisted herself onto the sink and looked surprised at Stella's expression and the squeeze Stella gave her knee. "You okay?" And when Stella nodded Gina said, "You sure don't talk much," and looked at Stella wistfully.

Stella nodded and put her rubber gloves back on, submerged her hands in soapsuds and sanitizers, groping for the next glass. "I used to," she said. "But I married a man who used to beat me for it."

Beside her, Gina startled and stared but stayed quiet. Outside, beyond the trash cans, snow continued to fall against the purple night.

"My name is Stella Stanhope, and I've been running for – I don't know, months? A year? My husband is Frank Stanhope, and he's a bully and a cheat and a liar. But I didn't know that when I married him all those years ago. All the lies we tell ourselves," she said and her voice sounded tired even to her own ears. She glanced at Gina, wondering if she'd be able to see through her now, if the charade was up, simply because she, Stella, was telling the truth. But Gina still perched, still looked like Barbie as she leaned forward, listening.

"All those lies we tell ourselves. They become our ghosts, haunting our lives. They become our lives, and we haunt the edges."

Outside the wind picked up and the snow flurried in a circle, catching the floodlight off the back door of the bar. Stella saw faces in the snow but they were faces of the living – Julie and her Ben and baby Christy, and Frank Jr and even Frank, back before disappointment and rage became the order of the day for him and she wondered if it sometimes surprised him as much as it did her. She saw her friends and her own family and her comfortable spots at the library and she knew she had run, truly run, and she knew she needed now to stop. And fight. In the snow she saw faces, people she'd never known, strangers from the bar she'd taken shelter with and she knew if she was haunted, it was her own abandoned life that sought her. She thought of everything she'd given up for one man, one man who had promised to love her forever and who had cracked her jaw and her skull and bruised her ribs and battered her kidneys. She'd given up her children, her home, her friends and her career for him, become a ghost unable to even haunt those she yearned for.

She had a right to her life. Frank did not. And she thought of the marker in the graveyard, the last marker in the current year and the name just starting to etch its way across the brass and she shuddered and gripped the sink.

Gina put a hand on her shoulder. "Okay?"

Stella nodded and swallowed and stripped off the gloves. "I've got to go home. People need me. I need them. I can explain it to them. I can get X-rays, proof."

Wide-eyed, Gina nodded as if Stella were making sense. "Don't let him hurt you," she said.

"That's exactly what I'm going to stop him from doing," Stella said. She untied her apron and looked at the girl, pensive and perched.

Gina's eyes were distant. "I think about going – on, sometimes," she said, as if afraid to sound like she was stealing Stella's thunder, but not wanting to sound content and staid, either. "But I don't know where to go."

Stella closed her eyes for an instant, saw again Gina's marker backlit with snow and the winter afternoon. She opened her eyes and smiled at the girl. "Yet. You just don't know where to go yet." She patted her knee one more time, motherly and reassuring. "When the time is right, you'll know where you're supposed to go."

She turned away then and went to find the owner and tell him she was quitting, which she didn't think would surprise him somehow, and then she went upstairs to pack her bags and go, snow and night and all those miles but she was tired of being haunted. She had a life waiting for her to reclaim it and ghosts to exorcize and a future to prepare for.

Stella stepped out the backdoor of Mac's Bar and turned toward the rickety uncertain stairs. She stopped at the top and looked across the alley toward the cemetery but it was too dark to see anything and there was nothing there to see anyway. She turned her back on the graveyard and the marker with the name just starting on it fell away in her mind as Stella went inside to pack.

She left the other mystery under the stairs, the cardboard box decaying in winter's chill, for the next tenant of the apartment over Mac's. She'd solved her own mysteries, and that was enough.

Tales of Eaglesnest is a twisted fairytale of the vicious variety.
The story originally appeared in John Benson's Not One of Us, #40 (2008), which
included work by Caitlin Kiernan and Sonya Taffee.
At the time I wrote it, I was both doing a lot of reading in fairytales,
and surviving my first attempt at Atkins-style diet
You'll probably see a connection.

She gathers them close to her in the big formal easy chair so clearly hers. No one else goes near it during the day when she's away. The children sit tucked up close on either side of her, one per leg of lap, and her arms circle easily round their shoulders. She is tall and slim with long limbs and dark hair and they are so small and oh, so skinny, bruised eyes and tightened mouths. Their hands go often to their stomachs, as if protecting something inside or stilling an unquiet ache. They sit inches from food— mouth watering child food, everything from pork chops to pizza to cake to candy– but they seem to have no appetites. In the evenings they sit like this, on her lap, in her chair, tucked into the circle of her arms and she reads to them from the Tales of Eaglesnest.

Outside tonight the wind blows, frantic like a dog left too long on a chain. The trash cans tumble in the driveway and on the roof a slate has come loose, rhythmically banging. Whenever the slate bangs the girl's eyes go round and her mouth opens ever so slightly but she has learned not to say it aloud. Not to invoke the rage by saying "Daddy" or hoping beyond hope he will return.

The slate bangs again, and she meets her brother's eyes, sees there the same pain and despair, longing and loss, and still the voice continues and still the tales drag on.

It was many years ago, before you were born, you or your father or his father at that, when my great grandfather founded Eaglesnest. A beautiful place, a gift for his bride, but a cruel place nonetheless. No one died building it but no one lived well after it was built. And into that home my great grandfather took my great grandmother. But she was smarter than he. She knew better than to marry outside her own kind, knew that his choosing her as his mate had doomed them both unless she chose to act. And act she did. She had the tomes, the lore books, the mysteries. She knew sacrifice and sacrifice alone to the right beings– deities, entities, demons, angels, scavengers, it didn't matter– only sacrifice and loss could save them and she set out to do just that.

Sky met earth and the day darkened past midnight on the morning the first of the children was born. Sacrificial lambs to the slaughter. She fed them and cared for them and started taking others in when she realized two would never be enough for her to find the key and unlock their salvation. She opened her home to homeless children and the townsfolk called her a saint. She spent her days praised by her neighbors, praised and loved, and her nights learning the rudiments of torture and sacrifice, what called to what, what drew the best. Blood letting, fire, knives, hanging, evisceration– she tried them all, finding at last pure denial that caused so much longing was best.

She shuts the book hard and fast, lets it drop to the floor in a shower of dust and torn leather and bits of velum. The girl has given in. She's reached for a piece of cheese, close at hand, absurdly close and utterly forbidden. Her fingers curl around yellow cheese and the knife flashes out, fast and accurate. She pulls back her bleeding hand. Shaken, knowing better than to cry. It's a shallow cut. She cradles her hand against her chest, reaches for her brother's hand. Her eyes never look away from the food.

"Now listen," the woman says and pulls them tighter and begins to read again.

That night Josh goes foraging, leaving Jill behind. They're too hungry, can't stand the pain anymore, but Jill hates being left. Their mother left them, all those years ago, and their grandmother came from Eaglesnest to live with them but only for a while. Their father left then too, Jill thinks, in a way. Once their grandmother was in the house, living in their parents room and Daddy sleeping on the couch, Daddy changed. When his mother started disciplining Jill and Josh he looked away, his face sad and empty. And then after grandmother brought them to Eaglesnest he started going away altogether, going away for real. He told them things would be better when he returned and at first he sent them letters and postcards from the road but now those have stopped or grandmother no longer lets them see.

Jill snuggles down in the bed. Her heart pounds so hard she thinks it must be audible. She and Josh always sleep the same way, Jill scooped around her little brother, holding him. That way should their grandmother stick her head in the door she'll see the clothes bundled and rolled within Jill's arms, Jill's back to her grandmother and everything under control. So far they haven't been caught but she hates it when Josh goes foraging and he refuses to take her because the first time she went with him she stubbed her bare toes and started to cry and he's afraid she'll wake the household.

There are worse things than grandmother in these walls. She's told them that and they believe her.

The door opens with the softest snick and Jill tenses everywhere. Worst of all is knowing someone is in the room and not whether it's Josh returned or her grandmother come quietly to watch them. Or grandmother come quietly to tell Jill her brother is caught, her brother is dead, her father died out on the road, her family is over and ended and through– the bed dips only a little under Josh's weight. He doesn't weight much.

"Jill, I got something."

And now is another worse part. He crawls back into bed and she wraps around him. His feet are like ice and she warms them against her legs. They lie still, pretending to sleep, counting slowly in their heads, making sure no one heard anything, no one followed Josh.

There's meat. No wonder tonight he took so long. Josh has been bold. He stole a piece of cold beef from under the foil in the fridge. There's meat and cheese and bread.

"I had to use the knife for the meat. I thought I might as well get the rest."

Jill doesn't answer. She concentrates on taking small bites and eating slowly. Eating too quickly makes them sick and it has been two days since Josh last foraged. He's brought mints and crackers and a perfect shining apple, things they can hide in the niche the back of the bedside table creates, a thin flat spot to hide things.

They've rarely had anything to hide. The last of the postcards from their father are back there, and a single curly photograph of their mother. Half a photograph. The picture shows her seated in a hardback chair, someone's hand on her shoulder but the rest of the person not in the picture. She is wearing a white dress in the black and white photo, and her hair is loose on her shoulders. The picture has been torn horizontally just under her rib cage. Other than the photo and their limited food, the spot is bare. Until tonight. Josh pulls out squares of chocolate, one each, less afraid of getting caught than of getting sick, and then he pulls out what he obviously considers the prize.

The Tales of Eaglesnest.

The book hits the bed with force. It's old and cracked and molding and heavy. Jill jolts back away from it, both hands going up in defense.

"What did you bring that here for? She'd kill you if she knew!"

Josh's eyes no longer look like a seven-year-old's. he blinks at her and sighs. "What is it you think she's trying to do to us now?"

Jill just looks at him for a moment, then quietly closes her mouth and looks down at the book, waiting for Josh to explain.

"She never lets us touch it," he says softly. He's sitting beside her on the bed and he's not touching it now, just looking. He looks as if he expects the book to move on its own, waking the household and alerting grandmother. They're not alone here– there's Gardner and Maid and Driver, and Cook who works for grandmother when she gives her elegant dinner parties, nights when Jill and Josh are fed until exhaustion sets in and food is repugnant. But there could be an army in Eaglesnest and no one could help them. They are here alone without their father. "Haven't you noticed? She never lets us touch it."

"She never lets us touch anything," Jill says and touches the cut on the back of her hand lightly.

"I thought maybe it could help us," Josh says. When she stares at him he says, "She so never wants us to touch it. I thought maybe it could help us."

Jill shakes her head. "It's just stories. Old stories. Mean ones." But she reaches out for it and opens the cover over their laps and together they read as night bleeds closer to morning. Before the sun is even a hint they store the crackers and mints and apple behind the table stand and then Jill waits for a second endless period, her arms close around the rolled clothes that should now be her brother in the few hours they have safe. But Josh returns undiscovered, slips into bed beside her and the sky is still dark and they still have hours before they wake to another day at Eaglesnest.

"Josh, where do you think Daddy is?" she asks and he says sleepily, "Getting help."

"My grandmother came from a family of twins," their grandmother says. The children are tucked onto her lap, her bony legs un-welcoming as ever. Josh has caught a cold and cannot forage for fear of sneezing or coughing and being caught. The food tonight looks especially wonderful, fresh hot pizza and mugs of cocoa. Jill never takes her eyes off it. Josh refuses to look, which angers their grandmother. She points them to it, frequently rearranging them on her lap. "But more than twins, listed each time as a single birth, grandmother learned to use live bait. Grandmother used her husband to protect the family. Her designs were beautiful, the webs of spells most lovely. There's a picture here, look, look at it, children." The tension in her arm says she is prepared to shake the children and force their heads down over the page. There is no need. They have been through the Tales of Eaglesnest backward and forward beginning to end. There is no horror they haven't already visited. The picture on this page shows a white skinned man, shirtless, back to the camera. His back is a maze, a spiral, a bloody red dance that drips down to stain his trousers, a red masterpiece of pain and fear. His hands, in the picture, are bound to his sides and his face is turned just enough for them to see part of his expression.

It is the same look of tired fear and defeat they see in the mirror every day.

"Grandmother, why do you do these things?"

Jill goes cold and still when Josh asks. She has put them off her lap and is putting away the book. Their evening time is over. Their bed time approaches. In a few hours they will eat their stolen food and Josh will go looking for more forbidden texts while Jill reads more in the Tales of Eaglesnest.

Grandmother stops moving also at his question, looks as if she intends to sit back down with them. Jill squirms. She wants away from her grandmother, away from the food. She wants to be back in their room while Josh forages, reading the book her grandmother has just returned to the shelves.

But grandmother doesn't sit back down. She stands facing them as a teacher might face a classroom. She looks angry but she answers, taking in both Josh and Jill. "There is a curse on this family," she says at last. "We do not marry outside our own kind. We are– unnatural. And when my great grandfather married my great grandmother he cursed our line. She was the one who started the book, the one who began leaning the ways that allow us to survive."

"Why?" Jill asks. She can feel Josh go totally still and cold behind her but she waits for her grandmother to answer.

"No one wants to die, little girl. This family is part of the weave of life."

It's not life, Jill wants to say. Not living here in this ancient house, subjected to the vagaries of her grandmother's torture. The mistress of Eaglesnest answers her as if she's spoken.

"You have no idea of what you do not see. Of what is beyond this house. You have no understanding of power."

"Make me understand," Jill says and she reaches for the pizza. Behind her Josh breathes <u>No</u> and her grandmother smiles, very slightly, before she moves snake-fast, pulling the food from Jill's hand, trying to force it from her mouth and when she fails she gives them both emetics that night. They huddle together on the bed, too weak and wracked with shaking to move. Josh cannot forage. He whimpers in Jill's arms. She tries to comfort him but her fingers curl away from his flesh, wanting to turn the pages of The Book.

She's getting stronger. Something in the book is making her stronger and when Josh complains about fetching it every night she stands between him and their stolen food, refuses to let him eat. He brought it to her, she points out, and sends him to fetch it. She used to hate the time spent waiting for him to return, terrified he'd been caught. She'd curl around his clothes to pretend it was him, just in case. Now she sits on the window box and watches the night sky. She is stronger now, but coming apart. When she peers into the darkness she feels it peering back. She sees the warp and weft of the night. She sees patterns in the darkness. She thinks when she understands them at last she'll be able to enter the darkness and at last she'll be safe.

"I won't go," Josh says. "I'm not getting the book for you again."

Jill's nails bite into her palms. She wants to scratch and pummel him but she's afraid of the noise she'd make. "I'll go myself, then," she says, and he tries to block her path, but only for a moment.

That night he waits as Jill has so many nights, sitting up in their bed, starting at sounds, waiting as his heart pounds endlessly.

It's a joy to be free in her grandmother's house. At first she doesn't even know what to do. Moonlight seems to shine in every window— there are pathways of light as if someone lights her way. Jill dances soundlessly, sure in her own silence. Fear has flown. She is no longer the little girl who stubbed her toe while foraging and whose little brother wouldn't let her accompany him. He's kept it to himself all this time, the wonder and joy and freedom of his midnight wanderings. She has never been able to adequately judge how long it takes him to return. Now she wonders with every room, every discovery– did he come here? Or here? Or here? But Josh– pale, frightened Josh– maybe he'd only ever got as far as the kitchen and later, after she started ordering it, the parlor for the Book.

Moonlight lights dark wood floors. Jill pauses at the living room, austere and empty, and at her grandmother's office, a dead, cold room. There is nothing there to interest her, at least not for now. What she seeks is in the parlor and she goes there, feet cold cold on icewood floors and the moon leading the way until the Book is in her hands. And she can go back now, through the kitchen, foraging as carefully as Josh told her to, cheese and bread and something to drink, they're allowed water, after all, but the Book sings to her and she settles in the parlor, in the river of moonlight, to read.

Time slips by. Jill rereads passages for the first time, discovers new ones ancient to her. She hears the floor shift and squeak and freezes with terror until the rhythm continues, just an old house in the night, unquiet sleep.

Dawn is graying the sky when she rises, cramped and cold, and slides the book back on the shelf, realigns the ribbon from the binding, replaces the single hair her grandmother has used as a trap. She tiptoes through the kitchen, takes chocolate and apples and slivers of beef and returns to their room.

Josh wraps around her and warms her icy feet against his legs.

"Your mother was a fool." Their grandmother holds them close, tighter than usual. Her bony legs feel like knives. The children want to squirm. Tonight there are barbecue ribs and marshmallow fruit salad and chicken wings, watermelon and garlic bread and ice cream. Summer must be coming but the thunderstorm outside the window belies it. The children's eyes go to the food but it's automatic by now. They hardly long for it. They have become adept at taking what they need, first Josh, then Jill, such skillful little thieves Cook finds nothing amiss in her proper kitchens. Still they look and sometimes reach. It wouldn't do for grandmother to suspect.

Tonight their grandmother holds them close, whispering her vile stories into their ears. Their mother's nightmare childhood races across their minds. There is nowhere to go. No way free of their grandmother's trap. Hearing her mother's name, Jill's initially calmed before she panics.

The stories are ending, winding to a normal conclusion. The pattern will shift when her grandmother finishes reading the Tales of Eaglesnest. She will choose other books to share with them. Jill has seen some of the other books– they are written in blood and they are not finished.

They wait for the blood of their next readers.

"We are running out of time," she tells Josh. They are huddled together on the window box, the storm outside scratching the glass and shattering the sky. Tree branches crack in the wind. "When she gets to the end of the Book, something will happen."

"Daddy?" Josh asks and Jill half turns to the door before she realizes what he means. Her anger is instant.

"Don't be stupid." She waits a heartbeat watching his hurt, startled expression, then says, "It won't be anything good."

Josh goes with her that night, the two of them prowling as she thought they always should have. In the parlor she ignores the Book. She is looking for something else. Josh follows her, lost and confused, until she rounds on him. "Back off. Don't follow me. Go back to the room if you can't help."

Josh's face crumples. He looks as if he's going to cry. Jill relents abruptly and holds him close, the way she used to. "We have to find Daddy's letters. We're running out of time."

The house shifts and Josh grabs her arm, hard enough to make her wince. The look in his eyes is enough to make her feel guilty for her anger.

He's just a terrified little boy.

But he's been foraging for months– surely he's heard the house settling in the night.

How terrified he's been. How foolish and scared. Those who live within the walls of Eaglesnest need to be made of sterner stuff.

The house creaks again and Josh breathes, "Grandmother," with such conviction and terror that she is there, for just an instant, within the doorway. Jill blinks and the vision is gone. She backhands Josh across the face without conscious thought, her hand across his mouth and his tears silent.

Jill turns away from her brother and scans the room. She is certain the letters are in the parlor, not in her grandmother's office. The parlor is the heart of Eaglesnest, where the Book is kept. Where grandmother reads to the children tucked up close in her lap. Where generations of family learned to counterbalance the curse upon them and somehow figured they were alive.

Jill's gaze sweeps the room. There. Beneath a shelf of books she has yet to explore, a cigar box stands in plain sight. Of course. It is directly across from the chair where grandmother holds them prisoner in the evenings.

There are letters at first, neatly folded within neatly slit envelopes, letters addressed to the two of them. For the first few months grandmother let them read the letters, their hope one more instrument of torture. Since Christmas they've received nothing. Now Jill holds a pile of envelopes in her hand, then postcards, brightly colored at first and dwindling down to the plain white cardboard bought in the post office moments before mailing. The pile is bound together with a black satin ribbon. Jill pulls it loose and something shifts within the house, as if something has changed or been set free. She pauses and looks around but nothing is different within the room. She bends her head over the letters and Josh squats silently beside her, reverent or afraid of her anger. She should reach out to him and reassure. She does not.

The letters are in order by date. The oldest tops the pile. She remembers the first letters. The stains on them may be her tears. The letters promised Daddy would return for them, he was searching for work, for a way to free them, he loved them and he'd be back. They were postmarked only a town or two over. He was searching close to Eaglesnest; he didn't want to be away from them.

Over the months, the letters changed. The postmarks were cities away, and then states. He was coming for them. He promised. Eventually. They should wait. Their grandmother would see to their safety. He'd be back.

The last postcard read simply, "I'm sorry."

There was a photo in the cigar box under the letters. Jill lifted it out gently and smoothed it on the floor. Josh reached for it and she didn't slap his hands away. He stopped without touching it anyway. "Mama?"

It was the same photo they kept hidden in their room, safe behind the bedside table where grandmother had never found it. Their cropped photo ended mid-rib cage, their mother's hands pressing downward and her expression open and surprised. They'd always wondered what she was expecting.

This photo was whole.

Their mother sat in an empty room in a hard-backed chair. Her hair was perfect, curls spreading over the shoulders of her white dress. The photo was black and white but Jill remembered the white dress just as she remembered the deep auburn of her mother's hair. Her eyes slowly left her mother's face, looked down. Her mother's hands pressed tight against her abdomen and her posture in the chair was rigid, knees pressed together and muscles tight enough to see even within the photo.

To no avail. Blood dripped from between her fingers, blood splattered to the floor, blood ran and fell and splashed from the edges of the chair, caught forever freefall frozen by the photograph and even though the photo was black and white, the blood was red. Red and warm and wet.

Jill brushed tears off the photo. She wouldn't cry again. She placed the photo back in the box and the ribbon with it but the letters she kept for no reason she could explain. She didn't want them bound again.

Josh was silent as she led him up the stairs and undressed him and got him into bed. Silent and shocked. In shock. Gone. Jill got herself into her nightgown and slid into bed and, for the last time, wrapped herself around her brother, warming him.

In the morning, everything is different. She goes downstairs for breakfast. Josh is too afraid to follow her and at first she tries to bribe him with all the things they smell in the mornings– bacon, pancakes, scrambled eggs– and then she simply leaves him, curled on the bed, and goes downstairs to breakfast.

Grandmother looks up from the table, expressionless. She has the newspaper spread before her, a half grapefruit at her elbow and on the sideboard the food stands in warmers. Jill's mouth waters. Pancakes, bacon, eggs, home fries. She makes herself look away and meet her grandmother's eyes and she nods. Hello. Grandmother's expression is almost amused. Or appalled. She returns the greeting and watches. Jill goes to the sideboard. One perfect setting is laid on the table– the fine china plate is on the sideboard. Grandmother isn't expecting company. Jill forces her shoulders to relax. The plate is gently warm in her hands.

"I guess you'll need to ask Cook for another plate," she says. She's proud that her voice doesn't shake. She serves herself a little of everything on the sideboard. She sits across from her grandmother and digs in.

"I guess I will," grandmother says at last.

At the end of the meal Jill cleans her plate as best she can, discards the napkins and stands. She'll fill the plate again, take it upstairs to Josh. Before she reaches the sideboard grandmother puts out a hand and catches her by the wrist.

"Those who live within the walls of Eaglesnest need to be strong," she says. She looks deep into Jill's eyes. Her grip on Jill's wrist is not unkind but it is firm. Jill stares upward toward their room. She bites her lip and at last relaxes. She places the plate back on the table and turns to go upstairs. Before she gets out of the dining room grandmother says quietly, "Why don't you go into the parlor and read some more?"

She knows, Jill thinks. *She's known all along.* And grandmother's words are a challenge. One she meets. She turns and looks back at her grandmother.

"Good idea," she says. She hates the way her voice breaks but her grandmother just considers and then nods. As if she's won.

As if they've both won, somehow.

Spring thunders into summer. Jill's clothes begin to fit again and her face in the mirror looks like hers. Josh forages at night and she hasn't told on him, out of respect for all the times he brought her food, but she doesn't attempt to take food to him. You have to be strong to live within the walls of Eaglesnest.

At the start of summer, their father returns. Jill is reading in the parlor when she hears the doorbell. She thinks nothing of it. That's what Maid does, and Driver. Someone answers, however, and she doesn't hear voices as much as she hears the silence, the sudden full silence and then the sound of her grandmother's shoes quick and hard across the tile but he must already be inside because she hears his voice from the hall just outside the parlor. She goes still. The book in her lap is warm as flesh, the pages red as blood. She hears Josh run screaming and now, at last, she hears her father's voice, a rumble, coming closer, and "Where's my girl?" he asks. "Where's your sister?" to Josh. He steps through the door into the parlor. Josh has hidden his face in his father's neck and so she sees just her father. She has an instant out rush of love at his soft brown eyes and flyaway hair and then, slowly, as she stands, she thinks how weak he looks. Fragile. Not strong. Like Josh, compared to her. Not strong enough for someone with a family in this place. Not strong enough to break the curse.

She finishes a note in the book and puts it carefully aside and stands. "Hello, father," she says and watches his face go wary. Grandmother is standing behind father and for the first time ever, Jill sees her smile.

Scare Tactics got started from a freewriting exercise on a glorious July day when I had Halloween on the mind. The very surreal story that came pouring out eventually found a home in Talebones #33, summer 2006. That issue also featured work by James Van Pelt and Nina Kiriki Hoffman. If I can have favorites among my own stories, this is one of them.

Scare Tactics

Autumn equinox come and gone and Halloween coming on fast. He still hasn't left her. Truth be told, the woman scares him to death. Came here as a handyman, looking for a quick fix of money and time. A little alcohol filched from the sidebar when no one is looking. Maybe some clothes if her husband left any behind. There's evidence of a man around the place. Or really, of a man no longer around the place. Little things, like tools stored in gasoline. A ladder too heavy for her to lift. Jack can't blame the guy for leaving– damn woman ghosts, flashes from room to room, appears like a bolt of lighting to make sure everything is being done to her satisfaction. Only she never is. Satisfied, that is.

Sometimes he thinks about what life was like on the road. Wasn't so bad, and it's not like she's given him anything. Can't actually figure out why he's staying on. He wants to leave. But winter's coming on in the Pacific Northwest, where if there's not drizzle, there's rain, and where there's not rain, there's snow and who knows what else. October's already set in hard with bright days and limitless nights and the smell of wood smoke so hard, combating the frost. Crisp you call days like these as long as you have somewhere to go at night. Otherwise it's just damn cold.

Still, he thinks about leaving, Jack does. He wants to. But there's always scare tactics. Soon as he gets to dreaming about leaving all of a sudden all his dreams are about leaving altogether, the scary kind of leaving. Almost like she knows, like she can get into his dreams. Or she'll just appear on his doorstep, just outside the behind-the-garage room she gave him, like she's reading his mind.

So he's stopped thinking about leaving, and started thinking about other stuff. Surface stuff. It's not really that hard. It's like white noise. Get to looking at a magazine or the television and underneath he's thinking about what he could do to scare her as bad as she scares him. Only sometimes lately he gets to feeling he's not alone in there. Like somewhere down under the white noise someone else is home with him. And that's scare tactics enough for anyone.

Bar's pretty much like any other. This one's of the Quaint variety, with a fireplace and easy chairs. Or maybe the fireplace is just necessity in this neck of the woods. There's a pool table, and a piano, although happily no one is playing it, and there's a long curving bar out of real wood. At the bar there's a handful of disenfranchised guys. Enough to start up a conversation. Bars are bars. Guys are guys.

There were introductions up and down the bar. Male names, all the usual. Bill and Bob and Mark, John and Kevin and Chris. No one's really going to remember them. Game's on. Late Sunday afternoon and the Redskins getting pounded. Outside the rain has started up again; looks to turn to snow somewhere around midnight.

"So you're the new guy?" Chris said after another round of beer and ads had gone by. "Up at Thira's place? Weird ass name."

"Ayuh," Jack said, general agreement. "She's an artist."

Scattered laughter came back. Like he meant something else.

"How long you going to stay?" someone asked. A Tom, maybe, or a John.

Jack shrugged. There were rigs in the parking lot. The clientele wore flannel. This wasn't a place people stayed.

"You know the stories?" the guy on his left asked but somebody else said something that ended with "artist?" at the same time and just down the bar someone said, "Holy shit, would you look at that?" and everyone's attention went back to the screen, to the pass and the run, 50 yards, and then they needed to order more beer.

The game didn't end so much as just ran out of stream. Late fourth quarter the score was so uneven it looked like time for miracles and not the right night for the miraculous. The bar cleared out in clumps, big truck motors turning over in the parking lot, gear up and off into the storm until it was just Jack at one end of the bar, bartender drying glasses, two guys at the far end still eating peanuts.

"An artist, huh?" the bartender said. Opening gambit.

Jack shrugged. "Said she is. Why she needs help around the place."

"So what's it like up there?" Casual question. The bartender was looking rather attentedly at the glasses in front of him rather than at Jack.

Who pictured it again, the way he saw it the first day. No wonder everyone wanted to know. He'd gotten used to it.

Big house, and dark. Even on that bright early September day it had seemed dark. Curling driveway through stone and iron gates, up to the house. She met him on the front doorstep, dwarfed by the ten foot door. Tiny little thing, in paint-splattered blue jeans and bare feet. Probably somewhere in her 40s like him, and hanging on to pretty.

"Mr. Tucker?" she asked and right away he said, "Call me Jack," but she didn't answer, just said, "I'm Thira Tompkins," and asked him to follow her. He called her Mrs. without asking if that was right and she didn't correct him.

She showed him the house with an air of finality, as if he were here now just to see and get acquainted but like she didn't expect him to return. Sterile was the word that leaped to Jack's mind. White walls with a lot of art and it was either hers or a favorite artist's because it was all the same hand. Nothing out of place in the house. Nothing even to be out of place. Kind of like she didn't live there. When she caught him leaning in close to a painting– red on red, brownish red– abstract, unless his eyes were going– she told him somewhat sharply to follow her. He got a good look at the painting right after she turned, though, and the paint had texture, thick and clotted, and it reminded him of something. Then she turned and said "Follow me" again, lead him out the kitchen door and across the dry summer dirt to her studio, and then to the garage and the room behind. His room faced southwest and got afternoon sun before the trees ate the light, and it gave him shudders the very first afternoon for no reason he could explain. It did, or she did.

"You heard the stories?" the bartender asked into his thoughts.

Jack's vision cleared; the bar came back into focus. "She needs somebody there to get the place ready for winter, dig her out to the road, chop firewood," he said in response to the question he thought he'd heard. His head buzzed, as if full of bees, and his ears rang. He'd talked about her too much. Conjured her, maybe. Something stirred inside him, and his vision changed. The bar looked overexposed. Jack blinked. Felt like someone else was sharing his eyes. Someone else. Something. Time to finish his beer and head up the hill, back to the house. Jack fingered his keys. Hadn't had enough for the bartender to stop him. Go out and start the remains of the Ford and off he'd go. Just for an instant he thought about starting the truck and heading as far away as he could get, but a wince of pain shot through his temples and he gulped beer, ready to settle up and head out.

The bartender was still waiting for an answer. Jack shook his head in response. "Stories?"

That was the cue. Bartender looked away from him, back at the sink. "People disappear," he said. He didn't say anything else.

After a minute, Jack said, "People do," but he wasn't certain if he was asking a question or arguing. He paid up and headed into the storm and by midnight the rain had turned to snow.

No white noise tonight. He stared at the TV but it was full of snow as the world outside. He kept it on anyway, just for noise. Just kept thinking about Ginnie and the girls tonight. Sometimes he wanted to go home so bad he could taste it, like blood on the back of his tongue. Could imagine himself on the front walk, the front porch, walking in through the front door and the girls would be there and—

—and in another couple months he'd be restless again and that wasn't fair to them.

Go to sleep, he told himself. Things will look better in the morning.

Yeah, right.

He had the last of the enormous paintings to hang and that would be it for the day, and snow or no snow, a cold beer was going to taste pretty damn good when he finished. Twilight set in while he'd wrestled the paintings. He was in some back room he'd never seen before, which wasn't surprising given the size of the place. No windows, just art, and she'd redone the room recently, he guessed— it still reeked of paint. Jack spent the better half of the afternoon putting it all together. Back ached, head ached, and he'd worked up a sweat. Backed off the last painting to see if it was straight— one of those bizarre prints of hers, something full of screaming faces and scattered color. Damn thing looked like real faces trapped under glass, screaming to get out. Gave him the willies and still staring, he didn't notice when she came in. Took a step back and ran into her and jerked like he'd just hit live voltage.

"*Ho*-ly—" He caught himself. She looked tired, he thought. Like she had when he'd met her. Dry lines stood out around her mouth. Her eyes were flat. "Sorry, ma'am. I guess I–" wasn't looking where I was going. Well, that was obvious, wasn't it? He'd been backing up. She might have moved. "Guess I'm almost done." He nodded toward the walls and the monstrosities that hung there but her gaze didn't waver from him.

"I guess you are," she said and ever so gently laid one hand against his forearm. Jack froze, a moment of searing ice and cold fire, and then she released him and nodded. "You do nice work," she said and he started to answer and realized he'd been dismissed.

His first thought was to clean up the tools, make some kind of comment, I'll just tidy this up, shall I– but he just wanted to get out of here and away from her and his arm had begun to ache.

He got as far as the door when she spoke again.

"Would you like– a beer?" She sounded tentative, somehow. First time he'd heard her sound uncertain. And all he really wanted to do was go back to his room, but he heard himself accepting, all the same.

"I love this time of year." She stood at the window, in profile to Jack, looking out, her arms crossed over her chest in a position he associated with corpses. She held a glass of wine in her right hand. The dark claret caught the light.

The room seemed dark for all the lights that blazed. Her studio, across from the house, set apart. Track lights picked out circles of white and shadow, and the air reeked of turpentine and oils and something like spoiled meat. It was the only place he'd seen so far he could say for sure she lived in. Sketches tacked to drawing boards. Canvasses, stretched and waiting. Half a dozen paintings underway. Weird things, as if pain and terror could be caught in color. There was one painting close to the windows in a spill of light that caught Jack's eye repeatedly. A portrait, he thought, but it shifted and shimmered when he looked at it, never still.

The beer was dark amber, and cold. Something imported. But the taste was off and Jack pushed it away and stood. Time to head back to his room. He thought maybe he was coming down with something. Thira didn't respond to his motion. Her gaze remained beyond the window.

"New Year's coming so fast," she said. "Only two weeks. A little more."

"New Year's?" His arm hadn't stopped aching. He rubbed at it without thinking and a shock of nausea ran through him.

"Celtic," she said, turning. "All Hallows Eve and November first,

New Year's Day." She stopped talking for a moment and just looked at him. "All Soul's Day."

Jack shivered. His arm felt hot and cold. The beer inside him was uneasy.

Behind her the painting seemed to move. Jack squinted. When he entered the painting looked like nothing but colors, light and dark. Now he thought it was a portrait, an unflattering representation of a very old woman. Jack leaned forward slightly in his chair, trying to see better. The woman's eyes caught his, so full of pain–

"I put a lot of myself into my work," Thira said but she still looked out the window. Jack risked another glance at the painting and without looking away from the window, Thira said, "Don't you like it?"

He jolted, and turned. She stood too close to him, within touching distance. Jack flinched and drew his arm close to his body. "What?"

"The beer. Don't you like it?"

He looked down at the table. The beer had gone warm and flat. It was too warm in here, that was all. Too warm, too close. "I think I better call it a night," he said, and rose so fast his thighs clipped the table and made it rock. "Think I'm coming down with something. Don't want to give it to you." He nodded, then, something he couldn't remember ever doing before, almost like he was withdrawing from royalty, and then he was outside and the air was so cold it made him cough. But it seemed to clear his head as well and he stood breathing deep for a few minutes until he noticed she still stood at the window and then he headed to his room.

Endless night. The sheet worked its way around his throat. He battled covers and quilt. The air in his room was icy but Jack burned with fever. The covers became sodden. The pain in his arm wouldn't let him sleep. Several times he woke and thought he saw Thira in the room. He gave up long before first light and found himself sitting beside the phone. He could call. He'd called before but he always hung up before she answered. Someday a man's voice will answer the phone, he thought. In the end he went and took a shower and spent the day splitting wood and mending a fence. Snow had stopped and the roads were clear again. Around five he saw Thira drive out and decided that wasn't such a bad idea. Head over to the bar, watch some TV, listen to some stories. ("People disappear." "People do.")

"Hey, you're still around," the bartender said when Jack took a stool and nodded at the beer the man pointed to. Good memory, this guy.

"Still around." Tried to smile but his arm still hurt and his thoughts kept circling around calling home.

"So she hasn't got you yet," the bartender said as he placed the beer in Jack's path.

"Not yet."

"Y'got girl trouble?" the man next stool over asked in a slushy voice.

"He's got girl boss trouble," the bartender said.

"Oh, *man*, don't get me started."

"Okay by me," Jack said and turned his attention to the television screen.

She was waiting for him when he got back, he was sure of it. Made it look like it was a happy accident (for her) that she was hanging around in the driveway and just happened to run into her handyman.

"I could use your help," she said when he appeared. "I wanted to move a couple things in my studio." She looked halfway between old and young again. Jack wondered if it was just lighting or tricks of make up.

"Any way it could wait for morning?" he asked. "I'm pretty tired." Because truth to tell he still had the willies from the last time in her studio and his arm was only just starting to feel better.

"Could if I was inclined to let it," she said. "It will only take a minute." Pause for the length of a breath. "Unless that's too much trouble."

His shoulders dropped a little. Like he'd been gearing up for a fight and just given up. She was paying him. He had a place to live. It wasn't like he had a nine to five. He nodded and followed her inside.

Her five minutes turned out closer to an hour and the last night caught up to him halfway through. Thought he'd kicked whatever it was he'd been catching but he was tugging a monster trunk from one end of the room to the other when the dizziness got him and he sat pretty fast, head down and breath coming uneven.

"I'll get you some water," she said and he wanted to say, Just let me catch my breath, but didn't have enough breath to say it.

Whatever it was inside of him started twisting upwards then and Jack forced it down. No idea what was going on but he thought it wasn't good. He had a sudden flash of Ginnie and the girls and then Thira back beside him, offering a glass of water with one hand and before he could move, her other   hand   went   across   the   back   of   his   neck.

Once when he was a boy, his parents took him to the ocean and Jack, who loved water, headed into the surf. But it was morning and there had been a storm during the night, and Jack ran into a jellyfish.

It felt that way now.

Jack howled.

"Oh, my goodness, I'm so sorry. This is a new carpet— I must have given you a shock?" She put the water down and offered her hands to help him up and Jack, disbelieving, let her. Her hands were cold and clammy, but nothing happened when he touched them. "I'm so sorry. I didn't realize you were feeling so bad. You should have told me."

Jack's head started to clear. The studio began to emerge from the confusion around him. He managed to stand and let go of her hands. The paintings around him looked bloody. Jack licked his lips. "I'd better go."

"Yes," she said and when he looked at her— really looked— he thought she might be about Ginnie's age when they had Jill, or maybe a little older. Maybe when Jackie was born. "You'd better go."

But Jack wasn't so sure anymore.

Awake all night, October knocking skeletal fingers along the windows of the little room. Outside his windows leaves blow dry with the sound of autumn, ticking against the windows, scratching at the door. Something out there wants in but there's already something inside. Jack sits up all night, too cold in this little room and too awake. The thoughts are not his, and they should terrify him, but the memories are his, warm and red. Ginnie and the girls seem very close again but he doesn't even look at the phone— she never answers anymore.

Daylight savings time gone and the days are even shorter. Leaves don't skitter against the windows because the rains have come, leaving them wet and dark. Thira paints and the bloody faces that scream up out of her canvasses now look a little too much like Jack for comfort. He heads over to the bar a couple times a week— he's a regular now— and when he comes back Thira always has a project she needs help with, something that will inevitably involve touching Jack at some point. Sometimes he wishes he could just hold out his arm— or leg, or neck, or cheek— and get it over with so he could avoid the moving of furniture or the climbing of ladders. That part, the cover part. Across the studio the old woman in the painting looks ever older and Thira ever younger and Jack ever weaker.

He thinks about leaving and his head aches.

***

Damn cold day. Halloween eve, perhaps– he's lost track. He woke so cold he didn't want to move and after a shower so hot it hurt he went downstairs into the basement looking for the furnace. He'd decided to leave during the night, between waking in the cold and dreaming of his family. He may go home. He may go on. He may disappear (people do, after all.) But he's out of here. Few more days. He's got a paycheck coming end of the week. He decided he's going to be warm until then.

Basement was full of stuff. Looked like anyone else's basement except for the number of discarded canvasses and stranded paintings. Jack didn't know for sure but he thought most artists just painted over discarded work; they didn't throw out the whole canvas. He stopped, then, to take a closer look at the work Thira might consider inferior. He'd seen what she liked. What she didn't like was better. The portraits looked real. The faces were identifiable. The eyes held expression. Uniformly, the expression was terror.

Time to go. Time to get out. Hell with the last paycheck. But he turns and there it is, so lifelike he can't believe it. Three-D death mask, and this is no representation but all that's left of some poor sod, heart and most assuredly soul. His own heart starts doing a startled jackrabbit thing inside his chest but at the same time something is waking up inside him, the something that shares his vision and shares space. Something that wants to scare Thira as bad as she's scared him and he thinks now he might have a way, might have an idea.

Ginnie and the girls grin redly in his mind.

Jack– maybe the absolute last of what is really Jack– holds his hands up, warding off the death mask and the paintings and the future. His hands look old, like they've seen 80 winters instead of 40, and that's Thira's doing, but it's not too late yet. It's not too late at all.

So handyman for just a few more days and he'll head home, see if there's anything there that needs cleaning up. That needs his attention.

Halloween coming on fast, and All Soul's Day, New Year's to some, and people disappear all the time, don't they? People do.

The idea for The Party Over There came from a stray bit of overheard conversation. I wanted to do something with the phrase and ended up writing a very complicated story that made very little sense but had several of the same elements that appear in this version. The second time I wrote The Party Over There I had much stronger imagery in mind. I sent it to a small press, Invisible Cities, which was putting together a ghost stories collection. It was accepted, and shared a table of contents with John Updike, Peter Straub, T.C. Boyle, Nicola Griffith and Louise Erdrich.

The Party Over There

Gordon knew she was dead the moment he entered the house. It wasn't any kind of evidence, nothing untoward or obvious. It was more her special kind of resonance that was missing, gone as if he'd imagined that it had ever been here, and now the house hung silent around him, carefully decorated with a sure professional touch, delicately set with crystals and luxuries.

But empty.

"Sylvie?" His voice was uncanny in the stillness, too loud. He expected the curtains to move with the force of it, the crystal to shatter from the volume. Gordon's fingers curled around the hardwood banister. He started up the stairs to the second floor. She was up there, of course, whatever she'd done, she'd done it up there.

He'd known something was up for the past few weeks. Something had changed in her. Her eyes were brighter and her step quicker and the depression had settled away from her. He'd thought she was on her way to finding religion or some such nonsense and he'd tolerate it, as long as she had the sense to keep it out of his way.

Briefly he'd considered that she might have taken a lover, but got away from that thought fairly quickly. She wasn't the sort. And she knew the consequences. Too well. Which was why he'd been glad the depression had lifted, that Sylvie's sad eyes were smiling again, although her quick, nervous movements seemed geared toward hiding something from him. Once he grabbed her, thinking she was hiding something from him, right there, in her hands, and he left her wrists bruised but there was nothing in her hands, just a curious little smile around her mouth. She hadn't cried out or protested.

His feet were on the stairs of their own volition. He wasn't sure he wanted to go up. Sylvie changed the house by her presence or absence. Now the Victorian seemed old and decayed, as though he walked a crumbling mansion, alone in the moonlight and haunted. Gordon shrugged off the thought. "Sylvie?"

The upper hall was empty. As it would be. Unlikely she'd be in the hall. Her room was empty, clean and lacy, in an ordered, neat way. She always knew where everything was.

He always knew where she was. She couldn't hide from him. "I'm coming," he said, hearing his voice drop. He tried to keep it light. Hide and go seek. Just a game. She wasn't running.

She knew better.

Except perhaps this time she had run, and beyond his reach.

The bedroom was empty, the room he'd shared with her until a few months ago, after one bad night, when she'd moved down the hall and all the demands, promises and gifts in the world weren't enough to draw her back.

He passed from her bedroom to the master bathroom. The door stood closed, a beacon, letting him know where she hid. He never allowed her to close the door, always insisted she leave it open. She was taunting him. Gordon forgot what he knew and stepped to the bathroom. The door flew open so hard it bounced back, caught him against the forearm he had raised.

He was hardly aware of it.

The bathwater was red. Sylvie's red curls dropped into it, the ends floating limp upon the surface, and one of her arms had slipped outside the tub, perhaps thrown there in a moment of fear. Blood had dripped from the jagged line along her wrist, drops of it marred the white bath mats where more than once he had taken her.

"Sylvie."

Her face was slack, eyes closed, mouth a little open. He could just see her tongue between her teeth. The bathroom was full of candles, their light flickering weirdly over her face, causing little movements that weren't hers.

"Sylvie."

He moved her arm, returned it to the edge of the tub, as if she'd laid it out of the water to cool down a little. The water was very warm. She hadn't been here long. Gordon reached over and pressed two fingers hard against her neck, unafraid of hurting her. The pressure sent her head rolling back against the porcelain. There was no fluttering beat under his fingers, no rapid quick breaths, no pulsing ebb and flow of life. he looked at her still face.

"Sylvie."

She'd gone where he couldn't follow, left him here, alone.

"Sylvie."

She'd left him. Gone away. Gotten away.

"Sylvie!"

The mirror shimmered as she slammed the door back open, threatened to crack as the door rebounded and he slugged it again. His footsteps were thunder through the house, pounding to her room, throwing back open the door there. Inside he grabbed the first thing he came to, an ornate, crystal clock he'd given her after the first time. It shattered against the wall satisfactorily, the wall gouged behind it as it fell, a nasty place of darker paint, chipped and scolded. With one hand, he swept the shining collection of cut glass and crystal from the top of her dresser, left a scatter of sharp-edged light on the floor. The pillows shredded under his hands.

She'd left him, run. Where he couldn't bring her back. She'd gotten away. She'd defied him. He heaved the mattress from the bed, upended it, threw it against the wall, knocking books from the case, cracking the window. He reached down again and then stopped.

Under the mattress, against the box springs, lay a book, wine-dark leather bound with gold, something fancy but inexpensive. His motion stopped and he dropped to the bed.

The leather was coarse under his fingers, a nubby texture. A gold fountain pen lay beside it so he wasn't surprised to open the thing and find her spidery, elegant writing.

"Sylvia Chase Newton," she'd written her full name, including maiden, banished from her usually. "Sylvia Chase Newton. My life." It was dated several weeks back, about the time the change in her began. About the time she'd started planning her escape, he'd bet on it. "Sylvia Chase Newton. My life." And the date. He took a shuddering breath. Not your life any longer. You messed up there. You haven't won, haven't won.

The first page tore under his fingers. Gordon struggled to control his breathing, turned the page to the first page of script.

"Gordon's tantrums continue, growing worse. I've stopped trying to do anything about them. I don't know what to do. My days would be so long, waiting for him to come home, except they're all spent on the house. Cleaning, fixing, bringing it to life. I don't know if he loves the house or hates it but if it's at all messed up – "

She didn't finish the sentence. Gordon tore the page, crumbled it in his hand. Bitch. Slut. It was all for you. Too lazy to understand. Had to be forced to keep up the house.

Another entry.

"Can't go out. Usually not my face, but lately—he's awful. The least little thing sets him off. I was trying to put aside some money, but he must have caught on and he took the checkbook. I don't know what to do. Ever since he killed Fluffy, I think I'd do anything to get away."

He couldn't see for an instant, couldn't see even when the room returned around him, couldn't see past the pain in his hand. Plaster lay on the floor, lacy chips of paint beside her dainty pillows. The book had resisted him; he could still read the words.

"Found a box in the basement today. Some previous owner's? Books on magic. Ready to scoff, but one of them is so old, and it looks real. It has all these crazy things in it, love spells and how to make a poppet, the appearance of the sleeping death and the hand of glory. And one of the newer books tells about scrying, looking for people or things through a mirror. Doesn't have to be a fancy mirror or magic or anything of the sort. Just a mirror. Like the one on the back of the bathroom door. Which actually is fancy, with that ornate frame, and I wonder if the person who owned the books ever tried it."

Bitch. Bitch. How often had she closed the door? How often to be so familiar with the mirror that shimmered there?

The book smashed against the wall, just to the right of the place the clock had made. The pages riffled as it fell, wounded birds found out on the creamy carpet. Gordon paced. One hand smashed the dresser and a few last crystal apologies fell, a bright sound as they hit the shattered mass on the floor. He stared toward the bathroom but he couldn't go in there yet. This, all this in her room, he could explain. Moments of grief. Overcome, officer. And the book would be long gone before the police came. But if he touched her –

The next entry was written five days earlier. Her writing was all over the place, excited curlicues dancing all over the margins.

"It works. The scrying. I can really see things in the mirror. A fog comes up and then—I found Tom. Tom, from college, who asked me to marry him, but I'd already met Gordon and he was so handsome and attentive, already taking the bar, driving a Porsche. And Tom, he wasn't ready to marry, wasn't even ready to have a career."

The pages bent and ripped and smeared under his sweating fingers. Found him how? Because she'd barely left the house at all, he'd seen to it.

And never would again, now. Remember. It's okay. She hasn't won. She ran, but she hasn't won.

"It works. The scrying. And Gordon is so into work, he hasn't noticed. It's almost okay right now, because he's not home. I was about ready to run, but he says he'll kill my parents and I believe him. But he's going to kill me if I don't—yesterday I was waiting for him to leave and thinking about coming up here to the mirror and he started demanding to know what I had and why I was smiling. I didn't have anything, just a book of matches to light the candles when he left, but he grabbed me and almost broke my fingers. After he left I came up and Tom was there. He's often with a group of people, Cindie and Jason, Kelli and Georgio, Kay and Dave. I feel like I know them. But Tom's always alone. And he looks the same. And I thought he saw me. Just for an instant. Shit! He's home—"

The writing stopped. Gordon left the book on the tumbled dresser, went down the hall into the bathroom. Among the candles were other things she'd taken there, incense, a short knife, some kind of herbs, a hammer, crystals. The mirrors were still steamy, the room humid from the heat of the bath water. Sylvie's head lay tipped to one side, as it had when he'd felt for her pulse.

Her arm had fallen into the water again but the bleeding had stopped. Gordon stared, thinking she'd moved. "Bitch."

He expected her to flinch, but she didn't move. Was she really dead, then? Truly run, actually escaped? Gordon slapped the door open. He couldn't remember closing it. For an instant the mirror shimmered, about to reveal something other than the bathroom, misty with heat, and then the door hit the wall. He thought about slamming it shut again, pummeling the mirror, breaking her door, stopping her escape. But that was crazy. Crazy as she had become. There was no escape, not from him. He kept track of his property. She hadn't run, she'd died. Packed it all in chasing a dream and was gone not won, not won.

"Dead. You're dead, Sylvie," he sad but he was already back in her room, down the hall, and he needed to call the police soon, the bereaved widower, and there was the rest of her carefully transcribed insanity to get through. He perched on the end of the box springs, and turned the next page.

The entry was dated for the day before. "Tom was talking about me to Kay and Dave. I know he still misses me. He said he thought he'd seen me, can't stop thinking. I know how to get to him. I can go through the mirror. It's dangerous, but I can do it. If I mess up, I'm dead. But if I stay, I'm dead. Gordon is going to kill me, sooner or later. I'm going through the mirror tomorrow."

He took a deep breath, trying to control the rage that crawled and coiled in his chest. He lashed out at the room, tore the curtains from the rods and left them shredded on the bedroom floor.

"Sylvie!"

The bathroom was no cooler, as if hotter water had been run. He thought she'd moved. He headed for the tub but movement behind stopped him. He spun as the door clicked shut, leaving him in the bathroom with her, and a mist was stealing across the mirror, a fog coming up and then burning off and there she was, Sylvie, laughing within the mirror, taunting him. She pointed, laughed, and when he turned fully to stare, she ran. Ran. Away from him. He couldn't see where it was she ran, only her feet hitting the ground over and over, only her form pulling away from him. He moved without thinking, grasped the frame of the mirror, and pulled himself through, thought he heard something in the bathroom behind him and then he was running, away from the mirror, after the bright flame of Sylvie's hair and even that was becoming dimmer, as if she faded.

"Sylvie?"

Her laugh came back. He ran harder, into nothing, into a nowhere world that surrounded him, a dim gray world, a flip side of their house, empty, gray and cold. A world where forever he would be walking up the stairs to find Sylvie dead.

"Sylvie."

"Here." The voice was behind him. Impossible. He spun, found himself facing the bathroom. She stood in front of him, wan and beautiful, framed in the mirror. He couldn't think for an instant, spun again, still looking. Impossible. "Sylvie, you bitch, let me – "

"Gordon," she said, clearly her voice. He stared out at her, at the bathroom behind her, the blood on her wrists, her hair, damp from the bath water. The cleverly colored bath water. The scratches on her wrists. He started forward. Bitch. He saw the fear rise up in her eyes. As well it should. He was only a couple steps from the edge of the mirror and this time she wouldn't be able to run from him. This time he was going to teach her a lesson she'd never forget. Good thing he hadn't phoned the police yet.

He'd hate to report a suicide before it happened.

"Gordon," she said again. Something in her voice stopped him. He looked at her again and she was smiling. "Gordon, I won." She stood in front of the mirror, blocking the exit from the gray world. Gordon ran, but he was still three steps from the mirror. She bought down the hammer and shattered the world.

I wrote "Cultural Differences" for the 2011 charity anthology "Healing Waves," edited by Phyllis Irene Radford for Sky Warrior Book Publishing, LLC. The anthology was a fundraiser benefiting victims of the Japanese tsunami that hit in March.

Cultural Differences

"I didn't think about bringing anything," Emily said. "I feel like such an idiot."

Actually what she mostly felt was very tired. They'd flown from Reno to San Francisco to Tokyo and while Matt seemed capable of sleeping through anything on the fight, Emilee couldn't.

"You've had a long day," Matt said, pulling her close against him as the train started up again. Emilee had a feeling the train might be faster than the plane had been. It was certainly cleaner.

"Look, we'll stop at a mall, you'll figure something out, Melissa will love it and she'll love you and all will be well."

"I love how your mind works," she said, relishing the arm around her shoulder. "Your mom hates me. Why should your twin sister feel any different?"

But he just kissed the top of her head and they sat and watched a trio of Manga school girls climb onboard, all lightened hair and darkly circled eyes and short skirts. They were followed by a harried mother, a look that apparently translated in every culture.

Emilee's eyes felt heavy. She refused to give in. Even if Matt's sister had married a Japanese banker there as no proof either she or Matt would be back in the country ever. She wanted to see it all, the amazing buildings and never-ending traffic that seemed caught in a perpetual jam. The white gloved traffic cops with their whistles and seemingly misplaced faith that some frustrated businessman wouldn't mow them down. The omnipresent vending machines. Everything came in vending machines here – umbrellas, bags from fancy stores the machines weren't located in. Bread. Everything came in cans.

What didn't come in vending machines came in convenience stores. They could probably buy one of the tiny cars in a convenience store and get insured from a vending machine and go join the traffic jam.

"Come this way," Matt said, and took her hand and tugged. Emilee followed happily through bright lights and clean slick floors. Nearly every store boasted English signs next to Japanese, but the store Matt led her to only had Japanese signs.

Em's eyes widened. A stationery store? She saw nothing but rows of cards, bright and confusing, and wobbled a bit from jet lag and exhaustion.

"But I need something to go with the card," she said, looking back at Matt. He couldn't wander away; she needed him to translate. He'd gone to university in Tokyo 10 years back, earned a degree in engineering and a fluency in Japanese she'd never have. Emilee was a freelance writer. English she got. Other languages escaped her utterly.

"They're not cards," Matt said, tugging her into the store where the colors swarmed around her. Row after row of staggered paper objects climbed from hip height to above her head. If they weren't cards, what were they?

Matt didn't explain, just looked delighted as she reached for one of the brightly colored objects.

It was an envelope. Nothing else. Just an oblong envelope, creamy stock, raffia ties and a pattern of brown and green frogs. When she opened it there was space for a very brief message, and nothing else.

Gingerly, Emilee put the frog envelope back and took a look around the other rows with their brightly colored off-staggered envelopes climbing ceiling-ward.

"OK," she said. "I don't get it."

Matt grinned. "Everything you could want is available here. In vending machines," he said and gave her an arch look.

"Watch it or I'll give your sister bread in a can."

"There are stores for everything and the Internet for everything else. So you can give specific gifts, OK, but you can also give money as a gift in Japan. As opposed to picking a gift card that ties the recipient to one store or brand, you can give money and let the receiver go where she wants. It's considered rude to just hand over naked money, though," and Emilee laughed at the image but nodded.

"Kind of like those cards grandmothers and aunts send birthday money in."

His turn to nod. "Except here the envelopes mean something."

"Of course they do," Emilee said, tired again, and realized she'd said it aloud.

Matt didn't look particularly offended so she risked following up.

"It's been a long day. I'd kill for Starbucks before we go to your sister's."

"That can be arranged," Matt said. "I'll help you pick an envelope and we'll go caffeinate you."

Only he didn't. He got her started in the right area, then promised to be back but went off in search of a restroom. Emilee tried not to let it bother her, standing alone in a country she'd only been in for a couple hours while she couldn't speak a word of the language, but she failed, and so she moved faster through the envelopes, flicking through them without really seeing them. She noted the time, repeatedly, and fluttered open envelope after envelope before deciding on the frogs and checking her watch again, feeling queasy with nerves. She glanced around, looking for the restrooms herself or for someone to help or someone to meet her eye, looking over heads of ex-pat Brits and Americans she didn't know and Japanese shopping for envelopes – and Matt.

"Are you all right?" He took her elbow as if she were about 80 and maybe a bit dotty and she sank into him.

"You are not allowed to go to the restroom again until we get home."

"This is going to be a long trip, in that case," he said, which made her laugh, and some of the tension drained away. "Let's get your envelope and get out of here," he said, without looking at what she'd chosen. "Train leaves in 20 minutes. Just enough time for Starbucks."

The train ride into the edges of Tokyo took Emilee and Matt through streets with gray rain pouring down and forests of umbrellas and intrepid cyclists apparently determined to go on about life despite the deluge. Slowly the view changed from city that seemed to go on forever to suburb, where houses seemed to be stacked on top of each other, bikes beat out cars, and the cherry trees were in bloom.

Emilee stood dumbly. The tired had caught up with her again and even Matt was starting to look a little dazed. Building in time to recuperate from the flight would have been nice, but between flights and Matt's work schedule, they'd arrived with just enough time for Emilee to meet Matt's twin, her husband and baby before the birth ceremony at the Shinto shrine.

Emilee yawned, her jaw cracking. "Why are we at a bank? Does Melissa work here?"

Matt blinked several times, like maybe Emilee was slipping out of focus. "Um. No. We need new bills for the gift. Did you get an envelope? I forgot to ask."

"I'll show you," she said, but inside the bank got distracted by the decor, the fast language coming from way too many people, the exchange of old yen for new and the fact that to the teller this was perfectly normal while to Emilee it was perfectly odd.

When in Rome, she thought, and almost giggled at the silliness of that and probably no one would have noticed if she had.

"Here, where's the envelope?" Matt asked when they stood outside again, and she pulled it from her purse at the same time Matt's cell phone rang and so she listened as he said in small bursts, "Mom, yes. We're here. No, just a short hop away. But we were coming to the house. So Melissa and Emilee can meet first. All right. All *right*. When did this get changed? Thanks for letting us know. Look, mom, I'm 35 years old and I <u>am</u> taking that tone," by which time Emilee had put the money in the envelope and put the envelope back in her bag and was standing watching Matt and laughing.

"Not funny," he said as he snapped shut his phone.

"It is when you're not on the receiving end for a change," Emilee said, smiling.

He one-arm hugged her, tickling her neck. Emilee laughed and squirmed.

"So I take it the plans have changed and now we're all meeting at the shrine?" She walked beside him, liking the sun on her face and the very different feel of the air.

"Of course." He squeezed her hand.

"And somehow the plans were always this way, or should always have been this way, or now are this way again because they just can't rearrange them just for us."

But they both knew Matt's mother meant just for Emilee and neither of them laughed and something golden faded out of the day.

The shrine entrance looked like a giant red letter A wearing a hat. Stepping through it the world changed from neighborhood to quiet. Carefully raked gravel, deliberately placed stones, beautiful greens growing in profusion. Emilee thought she could feel peaceful here, especially if they never located Matt's mother.

Matt suddenly sped up, tugging her after him, and she looked away from her surroundings and into the shrine and saw Judy holding Melissa's baby.

"Here we go," Emilee said.

Judy, tall, severe, sere, bottle beige, somehow, dressed in something outlandish either meant to represent high fashion or recent insanity, greeted them cheerfully, having passed off the baby skillfully before they got to her and sent Melissa and her father away so their coming upon her would look like a surprise Judy had orchestrated and so that the initial attention would all be on her.

"Matthew, this place is amazing. They have fish at every meal and you cannot get a good cup of coffee," she said within seconds, ignoring a variety of Japanese breakfast pastries and Starbucks on every corner, Emilee and Judy's own husband.

Annoyed, Emilee said, "We had a very good Starbucks before the train, and I saw six on the way here," which earned her the first of the stern, reprimanding and confused what-<u>are</u>-you-talking-about? looks from Judy.

Matt just squeezed her hand. "Dad, where's Mel? And where's my nephew?"

Jack grinned, gave Emilee a half conspiratorial glance, and led them to a secluded garden spot where Melissa and Len sat with a fat, gurgling baby that somehow looked almost as irritated as Judy herself.

"I am so glad to meet you," Melissa said, passing off the baby to her husband and giving Emilee a big, startling hug. Em, halfway to producing the gift envelope, fumbled the hug in return and waited on the gift.

The ceremony was brief, blessing the child in the name of the community god and again in the name of the sun goddess and again for the family, life and health. Emilee, swimming in tired, didn't know if the ceremony was traditional, fusion or varied by region. She hung back and watched and when the time came, presented their gift to the father, who intimidated Emilee because he smiled at everyone and never said a word, though his English when cornered was perfect. Quiet people made Emilee nervous. Of course, her mother-in-law was anything but quiet and Emilee assumed she'd make anyone nervous.

When she handed him the envelope, Len bowed, dark eyes leaving her

face for an instant, and untied the envelope with the profusion of frogs on
it. Emilee held her breath. Judy was nearby, talking with Jack about the
baby, and Melissa's attention on her child. Though Judy seemed distracted,
Emilee was sure if she'd created any kind of cultural faux pas, Judy's
attention would promptly be on her. Judy spent a portion of her Army brat
childhood in Japan. What she didn't remember, she made up, as long as it
made Emilee look bad.

Len opened the envelope, took in the amount of new, crisp yen and
the non-nakedness of the money, inclined his head briefly at her, and said,
"You have given him the gift of the future."

Emilee fumbled for words. Gracious would be nice but she had no
idea what the proper response was. "You're welcome," wasn't right, because
he hadn't said thank you in so many words. And with another wave of
tiredness, she said briefly, "I'm glad." She was. And maybe if her ways were
barbaric and American, at least people might understand her words and
actions were well meant.

She was too tired for anything else.

They walked the blocks back to Melissa and Len's home, Melissa
catching up to Emilee. "I don't know you yet – " She softened it with a
smile. "But you look really tired and no doubt everything changing didn't
help. Would you rather get a cab?"

Emilee felt tears behind her eyes, the tired encroaching and any
concern about her apt to tip her over into intense, possibly blubbering,
sentimentality. But she just shook her head at Melissa. The sun felt too
good, and the air, and getting a cab might involve close quarters with Judy.

"I'm good with walking."

Melissa, strolling now, surrounded by Emilee and Matt, said, "I am so
sorry about the last minute change of plans. I really wanted you to be able
to come by the house first, take a breather and then we'd go, and there
wasn't supposed to be any timeline. But my mother says she scheduled
something for after this, and so everyone had to move everything up."

She sounded as irritated as Emilee felt, which made Emilee perversely
feel better. She started to say, "It's not your fault, don't worry about it," but
bumped into someone on her other side and turned to find Judy had moved
up to walk shoulder to shoulder with her. The cold look in her eyes
indicated she'd heard. Emilee's stomach rolled over as if she'd just shot
down a high-rise in a super fast elevator.

I'll pay for that one later, she thought, and didn't question why she would and Melissa wouldn't.

Kneading her very tense neck that night, Matt said, "You know I'm proud of you, right? Not just for coming and dealing with my mother, but for getting the magazine to pay for articles on the flight and the trip." He kissed the nape of her neck.

"And writing off travel expenses," she grinned, comfortable. She's deal with Judy a hundred times over just to be with Matt.

Matt jogged off to the gym with Len the next morning and Emilee, who thought about retreating with book and coffee to the guest room, got into a conversation with Melissa about hiking the Tahoe Rim Trail at home.

Emilee, suddenly a little homesick, sat down and said, "Have you ever been up there when the wild flowers are in bloom?"

She'd met Matt on a hike interfering friends had set up and it had been the last time she'd hiked. Hiking wasn't her thing. But now, talking with Melissa about the Sierra, flowers and wide open sky, it sounded wonderful – half the world away and nowhere near Judy and Jack's home in New Jersey.

She was still in the living room, sharing stories of home with her husband's twin, when Judy came in.

Emilee's stomach sank. Just be nice, she told herself, and then finished: and escape, ASAP.

But Melissa defected. "Can you two watch him for a few minutes? I was going to wait until Len got back but I just want a shower so much."

"Of course," Emilee said automatically and since that was her own point of view, tried not to bristle when Judy said, "I'd be glad to watch him," as if Emilee weren't there.

Emilee gave her mother-in-law a perfunctory smile and a wide berth, moving around to the far side of the bassinet to attempt interest in the baby, their shared ground. She actually didn't care much about babies one way or another, but having offered to watch a new one, at least she could now pretend to be engaged in doing so and leave the conversation or silence to Judy.

Judy took the conversational ball and ran with it. Emilee tried not to blink. Sleep had been nice but she still felt off kilter, vulnerable to nasty jabs as she might not have been at home.

"You have such beautiful hair," Judy said musingly and Emilee smiled her thanks, waiting. "But I've always felt a woman of a certain age should cut her hair, don't you?"

Umm, Emilee thought. Am I now being invited to partake in these abusive conversations? And then since there was now a conversational hole for Emilee to throw her own ball into, she said, "What's a certain age?"

Judy looked smug. Her eyebrows always looked too high and arched; now she looked like a llama staring down her long nose, contemplating just exactly where to spit. "Thirty. Maybe thirty-five."

There, Judy seemed to say. Dodge that conversational ball.

OK, thought Emilee. "Oh. So young. I always thought women with beautiful hair – " she paused and let Judy decide whether or not Emilee meant herself – "Should keep it long until they're actually <u>old</u>." And left Judy to assume Emilee meant her.

"I'm glad we have a couple minutes alone," Judy said, folding her hands together primly and watching the baby as if at any minute it might get her dirty. "I've been wanting a chance to talk with you alone."

Speak, Emilee, or she'll leave it at that and your own imaginings will give you nightmares.

"And here we are," she said with the artificial brightness of a tour guide who's come to loathe everyone on her bus. "What did you want to talk about?" More grandchildren and when they could be expected (never, but thank you for asking). Is that really how you do your husband's laundry? It's disgraceful! (Actually, he does his own because he was so used to it before we married. And I think he looks great.) Diet, personal appearance or that at 35 Emilee was much too old to still be wearing her hair long.

She thought she was ready for anything.

"I wouldn't say anything, but I know that Matt will never say anything himself. He's far too well raised for that."

Emilee felt her eyes go wide before she could stop them. Yes, bravo, you did a *wonderful* job raising Matt. Possibly you could stop now.

Judy seemed to be considering her next words, possibly deciding how best to compliment herself and insult Emilee at the same time. "It's about this little – do you call it a job or a hobby?"

She looked at Emilee with the bright, avid eyes of something malignant about to pounce.

Emilee's teeth snapped together and refused to pry apart again. She gritted, "Do I call *what* a job or a hobby?" and almost any human on the planet would have heeded the warning and backed down or even skulked away.

Which made Judy officially not human.

She fluttered her hands, as if the distinction was a trifling matter. "The writing thing that you do, dear."

Emilee's breath and words caught in her throat. Her mouth opened, but nothing came out.

Judy continued. "You see, dear, Matt would never say anything, but he's used to certain standards in his home. If you were able to turn your attentions to keeping his home, maybe you could get a part time job as a secretary. Or you could teach." She looked as if this idea had just come to her. "That way when he came home from working all day he'd have the quality of care he's used to and deserves."

The world circled, nauseatingly fast. Emilee stood, fists balled, unable to stay still. Rage boiled. Her words came back in a rush.

"You evil, interfering, malignant, dried up old woman! How dare you? You never worked a day in your life, you have no idea what it's like to be prized for your talents and hired because you do something well. You have no idea what Matt wants in our marriage or how proud he is of me. You think I'm not good enough for your son and you want to see us apart because you don't want anyone else with him. Well, he loves you. Of course he does. He *defends* you and your words and actions enough. But you're his mother by default. He *chose* his wife."

Judy rose, smooth as an automaton. Her breath cold, she hissed, "How *dare* you talk to me like this?"

Emilee, refusing to be subordinate, said, "How dare *you* speak to *me* like this? We've been married seven years. That's seven years of your comments and shared oh so sorry about this confidences and I. Am. Finished. With it."

Sudden motion at the edge of the room distracted her long enough that she didn't expect the other, closer motion.

Judy slapped her hard across the face at the same time Matt came fast across the room. He caught his mother's wrist and dragged her roughly away.

"What the hell's going on?"

Melissa, on the other side, hair wet from the shower, robe pulled on cockeyed, said, "I heard some of it but I couldn't get out here any faster."

Matt turned to look at his sister, who said, "Judy decided to lay down the law for Emilee about everything she should or shouldn't be doing for *Judy's son*."

Emilee's breath was still coming hard, her stomach muscles fluttering as adrenaline washed away. She felt week, exhausted and angry. Looking at

Matt, she saw him close his eyes briefly, a look of pain and irritation, anger and sadness that scared her, because just for an instant she wasn't sure whose side he'd come down on. She felt alone and adrift.

Then Matt opened his eyes, let go of his mother and bridged the gap between himself and Emilee. He took her hand.

"What's wrong with you?" he asked Judy. "Can't you ever be happy for anyone unless everything that makes them happy is your doing?" Turning his back on his mother, he looked at Emilee. "Are you OK?"

She nodded, not trusting herself to speak just then. Tears of joy kept backing up in her throat.

Matt put his arms around her and she buried her head against his chest.

From beyond the circle of his arms she heard Melissa say, "I want you out of my house, mother. This is not the atmosphere I want for Ben. You can see him again before you and daddy leave, but not here."

Emilee could feel, "Oh, no, don't throw your mother out of your house," rise up inside her but she swallowed over it and waited, holding fast to Matt, until she heard Judy's footsteps crossing the hardwood floor and the door opening, and closing behind her.

Dinner conversation that night had a lot of twin speak in it that left Len and Emilee looking at each other in bemusement. Emilee came to like Len a lot by the time they set off to a cake shop in search of dessert, especially since though his natural reticence stopped him from ever saying so directly, she got the distinct feeling he couldn't stand his mother-in-law any more than Emilee could.

The restaurant was warm. Windows looked out on a beautiful spring evening. Melissa held Ben in a sling and checked on him and patted him naturally throughout the meal as if she'd been a mother forever.

Emilee, maybe because everyone was on her side, began to feel some mysterious remorse.

Overlaid by the angry dry towering perfectly coiffed woman who had risen to tell Emilee everything she did was wrong, to demand she give up her career to stay at home cleaning house, the way Matt had never even hinted he wanted, was a scared, lonely woman who'd never had a life to give up and who feared now the children were raised and the house downsized, her importance was finished.

Which didn't mean for even an instant she wasn't hateful or that Emilee ever wanted to see her again.

They strolled through the warm evening, poking into bargain shops and convenience stores because Emilee was still fascinated by the things she could buy there. They wandered into a bookstore where people simply stood for hours, reading, not buying, and into the cake shop for a lemon soaked confection they'd take home and have with coffee. No one much mentioned Judy and no one much didn't and Emilee wasn't thinking much about her until they came upon an envelope store.

"Uh oh," Matt said. "We're about to lose Em."

"New interest?" Len asked as they filed inside and Matt said for her, "New obsession." Teasing. Grinning.

"Not true," she said. "But come on, it's an entire store dedicated to envelopes." She went past him into the aisles, wanting only to see. An idea was slowly building. Melissa took Ben off to a quiet corner, and Matt stepped outside the shop with Len, who wanted to have a cigarette.

Emilee looked at the envelopes. This store, which for all she knew was the one she'd been in before, was also all in Japanese, but the colors and photos helped. She searched for a message: I'm sorry. Or I understand. Or maybe something that addressed the future: Long life. Prosperity. Good health. Those from what she could tell were very close to the wedding envelopes which, and she found this a little creepy, were very close to the funerary envelopes.

They were all beautiful. She couldn't very well get Judy a wedding envelope, or even an anniversary envelope, since she was never sure when it was. But she could get one of the positive, going forward envelopes, one of those located just beside weddings and funerals.

"Hey," Matt said, poking his head around the aisle she was in. "Don't want to rush you but Mel wants to get the baby home. You almost done here or should we follow them up?"

Screw it, Emilee thought. The evening was beautiful, she was enjoying the company and her mother-in-law would remain hateful despite the gesture and the careful attention to detail. The choice of envelope was all about Emilee, not Judy.

"Just let me go pay," she said, and chose one of the elegant envelopes she'd been contemplating.

The cards were really meant to dress up money. But Judy was now American as Emilee, and Emilee wanted the gesture to make sense. The next morning Judy and Jack were headed back to the states, a day before Emilee and Matt. The family met for breakfast at Melissa's, cooed over Ben, drank coffee in the warm sunlight and talked. Emilee waited until all the men had wandered off somewhere in the house and Melissa was suitably concerned with Ben before she approached.

Judy's lips tightened when Emilee came over to the sunny couch where she was turning the pages of a Japanese language magazine but she didn't speak or bother to look up.

Emilee took a breath. *It's not so much for her as it is for you. So you know you tried.*

She sat down beside her mother-in-law where she could only be ignored by direct rudeness, and handed her the envelope. Inside was a calling card, more easily found for American phones that Emilee would have thought. Truly she could find anything in convenience stores.

"I wanted you to have this," she said, and wished she'd spent less time on the envelope and more time on what she was going to say.

Judy fingered the envelope. She didn't say anything, but her light touch on the thick beautiful paper did. She untied it, studied the brief and noncommittal message – for a writer, Emilee had found herself shockingly out of words for both inscription and presentation; she just knew apology was out – and turned the phone card over in her hand. And Emilee, who'd meant Judy and Matt should not lose touch, understood then if Judy used it to call Melissa for baby updates, that worked too. If she used it to call Emilee – well, Emilee would deal.

They'd be short phone calls anyway if she didn't start coming up with words again. She watched as Judy studied the card and nodded, to herself, and finally looked up and met Emilee's eyes.

"Thank you," she said.

If it wasn't the start of a beautiful friendship or the uniting of two former enemies, it was, at least, detente.

There was a small whirlwind of activity before Jack and Judy had to go to the airport. Suddenly Judy, tearful, needed both Mel and Ben to go with her. Eventually Len volunteered to stay behind at the house and Judy was convinced to say goodbye to the baby there, and Matt and Melissa went with Jack and Judy to the airport.

"Can I tidy up a little?" Emilee asked Len as the car pulled away from the house and she took her first deep breath in days. Melissa's home was nearly spotless, but a baby and Judy's guest status meant surface clutter.

"You shouldn't feel you have to," Len said, noncommittal, and Emilee chose to consider that permission. She took a tray of coffee cups to the kitchen and returned to find Len holding the envelope with a horrified expression.

"Oh, shoot," she said, without thinking, and started to ask about the phone card, but the envelope was open and empty. Clearly Judy took the goods and left the point.

You did it for you, to be a better person, Emilee reminded herself, with just a trace of gritted teeth. And then, before she could say, "I got that for Judy because" and come up with some kind of because, Len looked at her, face troubled.

"I did not know there had been a death in the family during such a special time."

Emilee felt her blood chill. "What? No. I got it for Judy. It was in the life and celebration section!" Her hands moved uselessly, trying to change what he'd said. Len was Japanese. He'd know.

Len's eyes found hers and Emilee knew before he said anything this was more than a cultural faux pas, more than an insult.

"Tell me you didn't give that. Not for Judy. Not for anyone." He still held the envelope, but now out and away from him, as if it were contaminated.

Emilee stuttered. "I got it for her because of the fight. I wanted something, nice, a gesture. I gave her a phone card. So she could stay in touch with Matt!"

Len shook his head, upset. "She must not use the card to call Matt or Melissa or anyone! Judy grew up in this country – I cannot believe she's forgotten!" He stood, looked down at the envelope still in his hands, and threw it onto the floor. "To give a funerary card to the living. It is a curse. Any part of the gift inside will curse whoever is touched with it."

Emilee's mouth started working. "A curse? What kind of a curse?" As if perhaps there could be levels, variations of cursedness. Or as if she didn't already know exactly what Len was going to say.

"A death curse."

Emilee tried Matt. Len tried Melissa. Neither answered. But their mother was with them. She wouldn't be calling them. So for the moment –

And then Len's phone went off in his hands and he was talking fast, lots of "find her" and "get it back" and "Emilee didn't know" and Emilee was trying to get Matt, he had to be with Melissa, didn't he? But he wasn't answering.

And then she stopped. Because the phone was ringing in her hands.

The display read, "Tokyo airport," and below that, "Phone card: Judy."

"She knows," Emilee said quietly, looking at the ringing phone. Her mother-in-law knew. She'd left the death envelope behind and taken phone card. She knew, and she was calling Emilee.

Jennifer Rachel Baumer lives, writes, runs and procrastinates in the Northern Nevada desert where she lives with her husband and cats in the rural North Valleys, surrounded by jackrabbits, cottontails, coyotes and quail… and possibly ghosts.

Her work can be found in genre magazines and anthologies, both virtual and print, and in the previous collection The Last Oracle & Other Ghostly Tales, available through Amazon.
She also maintains a rather hit or miss blog at
http://jenniferrbaumer.blogspot.com/

A lonely woman in a surreal city haunts her own life.
A new house in a new neighborhood reveals its ghastly secrets.
And the grimoire discovered in the local used bookstore proves to be more than just a curiosity.

How clear is the line between life and death – or between the living and the dead? What happens at the Renaissance Faire when death in the form of the Danse Macabre doesn't pass by?

In this collection of nine haunting tales, award-winning author Jennifer Rachel Baumer reveals the secrets of the dead, and the ghosts of the living.

Available through Amazon and Barnes & Noble.

Two young seekers looking for knowledge in the City of Answers come perilously close to dying for truth.

A woman fighting to remain sane in the face of insanity finds the cure is worse than the disease and the end doesn't always justify the means.

In two stories of sacrifice, one woman learns just how hard change is and that progress comes at a price, and a young couple have to decide if the good of the many truly outweighs the good of the few – or the family.

And in the title story, a group of friends learn just what's behind the locked door that offers questionable refuge from the rain.

In this collection of six urban horror stories, award-winning author Jennifer Rachel Baumer looks at the horror found within cities – and within the people inside them.